Beauty

Beauty

Nancy Butcher

SIMON PULSE

NEW YORK   LONDON   TORONTO   SYDNEY

SIMON PULSE

An imprint of Simon & Schuster Children's Publishing Division
1230 Avenue of the Americas, New York, NY 10020
Copyright © 2005 by Nancy Butcher
page vii: from "A Spring Night," by Sara Teasdale
All rights reserved, including the right of reproduction in
whole or in part in any form.
SIMON PULSE and colophon are registered
trademarks of Simon & Schuster, Inc.
Designed by Tom Daly
The text of this book was set in Guardi.
Manufactured in the United States of America
First Simon Pulse edition April 2005
2   4   6   8   10   9   7   5   3   1
Library of Congress Control Number 2004105856
ISBN 0-689-86235-0

For Amy Durland

I am deeply grateful to Julia Richardson and
Nina Collins for making this book possible. I am
also grateful to Deb Sfetsios, Jayne Tsuchiyama,
Samantha Schutz, and Matthew Elblonk for
their contributions. And as always, thank you to
my wonderful family, Jens David Ohlin
and Christopher Reynolds.

I

❖

O beauty, are you not enough?
—Sara Teasdale

1

❧

QUEEN VEDA, THE SECOND MONARCH OF THE ROYAL kingdom of Ran, stood inside her enormous closet and surveyed the contents.

Her dresses were organized by occasion. On the left were the ones for affairs of state. Next to them, evening clothes. Then day clothes, then hunting clothes, then clothes for brisk exercise.

The dresses on the far right were for funerals and executions. She took one of them off its hanger and examined it. It was a long, wonderfully soft gown made out of black velvet. The collar was pure fawn, and the buttons, onyx inlaid with rubies.

The queen held the gown up to her body. The onyx was the color of her long, shiny black hair; the rubies were the color of her lips. She ran her fingers over the fawn collar.

She turned to the Beauty Consultant, who was sitting on his favorite stool. He was plucking apart a long-stemmed red rose.

"Well?" she demanded.

But the Beauty Consultant was engrossed in his rose. He was a tiny man, no taller than her dressing table. He had a shriveled bald head and hooded black eyes. The queen was not sure how old he was—perhaps a hundred, perhaps older. She had inherited him from her mother, the Lady Despina.

Momi. God rest her soul, she thought.

Or maybe not.

The Beauty Consultant was still absorbed in dismembering the rose. There were red petals scattered all over his lap.

"Well?" the queen repeated, irritated.

The Beauty Consultant barely raised his head. He regarded the queen from beneath his hooded eyelids. His black eyes glowed silver for a moment, then turned bright green. The queen smiled a slow, satisfied smile. The colors never lied.

"Yes, Majesty, most becoming," the Beauty Consultant whispered. He held the nearly beheaded red rose up to his mouth and nibbled delicately on a thorn.

Queen Veda returned the black velvet dress to its hanger, stroking the collar one last time. When was the last time she had worn this dress? Oh, yes. Galen's funeral. And just before that, at the funeral of Galen's young friend, Jana or Jaffa or whatever.

"The pink one, Your Majesty!" the Beauty Consultant whispered, startling her.

The pink one. Queen Veda ran her fingertips across her dresses, searching for it. All her dresses were lined up neat as soldiers: black silk with gold brocade, brown taffeta, emerald green satin, red mohair with matching cape.

Ah, there it was. The pink lace gown was the only item of pink clothing she owned. It was a daring shade for her to wear, at her advanced age of—anyhow, it was a pale, delicate pink, the color of a young girl's blushing cheeks. It was a color she herself used to favor as a young girl. Galen had liked it on her, and of course, before Galen, the other ones.

Queen Veda held it up to her body. The lace was so delicate: wisps of pink thread engaged in a gossamer geometry of flowers, birds, hearts.

She smiled at the Beauty Consultant, waiting for an answer. He was flinging the rose petals off his lap, one by one, and muttering in his strange language which she had never understood:

"Desse ciara treffen du mara."

"Pay attention!" the queen demanded.

The Beauty Consultant stopped muttering and stared at her. His eyes turned briefly cloudy, then settled back into their oily, inscrutable blackness. The Queen felt a rush of something unexpected—disappointment, rage. She gave a snort of annoyance and jammed the gown back onto its hanger.

"It was your idea," she muttered.

There was a ripping sound. One of her long fingernails had caught on the lace and torn part of the neckline.

The queen was about to extract her fingernail when she noticed that the Beauty Consultant's eyes were glowing red. Fueled by the compliment, Queen Veda continued ripping, ripping all the way down the bodice.

It was so easy. Pleasant, even.

When she was done, she was breathing hard. Her fingernails had dug into her palms, piercing the skin. But it didn't matter. The Beauty Consultant's eyes told her what she needed to know. They were the color of fire, of the fallen rose petals, of the blood that streaked her hands.

"Yes, it is you. It has always been you. And it will always be you," the Beauty Consultant whispered. "Your Majesty!"

Yes, yes, yes, she thought.

A magnificent sense of calm washed over her.

2

❧

PRINCESS TATIANA ANATOLIA, DAUGHTER OF QUEEN VEDA, sat cross-legged on her velvet window seat and stared out at the royal garden. Snow fell softly on the land-scape, obscuring everything in pure white: the gnarled rosebushes, the glass conservatory, the stone fountain. The winged boy with the permanent snarl was spitting a long, thin stream of ice.

Ana, as she was called, reached down and scratched her toes. The nails on them were long and ragged. She studied their peculiar color—black, with ripples of green and yellow—and marveled at their sheer ugliness. It had taken a long time to get them that way.

"Ana."

The door inched open, and Omi entered. Her pale golden hair was piled in high curls on her head, and the gray wool dress she wore looked wonderfully soft and cozy. *How nice it would be to curl up and sleep in it,* Ana thought. She hugged her knees and rocked back and forth.

Omi pushed the door closed with her hip. She was carrying a silver tray. "I brought you fruit."

Ana shook her head. "No, no fruit. I asked for pastries."

Omi set the tray on a table. There was a large bowl filled with apples, pomegranates, and orange blossoms. The fruit, Ana knew, had been grown in the conservatory along with the queen's winter flowers and her special beauty herbs. Next to the bowl was a curved knife and a white napkin embroidered with the queen's royal crest—a peregrine falcon, a tangled vine of roses, and the initial *V* in old Innish script.

"Child, you have been eating nothing but pastries for many moons now," Omi scolded. "You need fruit. Or else you will—"

"—grow even fatter than I am?" Ana finished.

Omi frowned. Her blue eyes, which were so pale that they looked almost transparent, regarded Ana with a mixture of anger and worry. Omi had been Ana's wet nurse when she was born. To this day, the soft almond smell of Omi's skin evoked in Ana a primal memory of feeding. The smell of her mother's skin did not have that effect on her at all.

"Tatiana Anatolia, why are you doing this to yourself? To the queen?" Omi demanded.

"Why, has she said anything?" Ana asked with interest.

"No. She hasn't. But how do you imagine this looks for her, how she must feel, having her only child neglect herself like this?"

Ana burst into laughter. "Bring me the pastries, or I will not eat anything at all."

Omi opened her mouth to say something, then clamped it shut. She turned with a sweep of her gray skirt and headed for the door.

"The cloudberry ones, and the ones with bitter chocolate!" Ana called after her. "Half a dozen of each. Or I will tell the queen you have been disobedient!"

The door closed, not gently. Ana stopped laughing.

A branch scraped against the window. The snow was falling harder now, so that the garden was all but invisible. Ana could just make out the glass walls of the conservatory and a single figure inside, moving around by lamplight.

Is it her? Or is it that nasty little man? Ana wondered.

The lamp went out. The conservatory and the person inside it blurred and faded into white.

Ana leaned back against the velvet pillows and stretched out her legs. She reached over and picked up the silver knife from the tray.

She turned it over and over again in her hand. The blade was so shiny, so perfect. She imagined peeling an apple with it and letting the skin coil into her mouth. Or slicing a pomegranate in half and exposing the slippery red seeds.

Ana used to love apples and pomegranates. She used to love orange blossoms, too, with their honey-sweet smell. Omi knew all this. But none of it could touch Ana anymore.

She ran one finger across the blade of the knife and felt the sharp, sudden sting of blood. Then she took a lock of her long golden-brown hair and ran the blade across it. Shreds of hair sprayed across her lap.

She sliced another lock, and then another, and then another. She could not see what she was doing, but that was good. Soon her hair would be as hideous as the rest of her.

3

❦

FOUR YEARS AGO, WHEN ANA TURNED TWELVE, THE QUEEN organized a party for her, as was her annual custom. Everything about the party was lovely: the ballroom adorned with rose and plumeria trees, the wild butterflies flitting through the air, the actors from Catonia performing elaborate dream-plays and shadow dances. Hundreds of dignitaries and royals were in attendance, along with the most important citizens of Ran. They drank copious amounts of wine out of silver goblets and ate tiny, perfect confections shaped like jewels.

The queen had had a red velvet dress made for the occasion, for Ana. "You are not a little girl anymore, darling Tatiana," she had said to Ana before the party, as she helped her on with the dress. "You are almost a young woman."

"Yes, Momi."

"You must make me proud tonight!"

"Yes, Momi."

Out in the ballroom Ana watched her mother mingling with her guests. The queen was dressed in a green silk gown that rustled stiffly as she moved. Ana thought that she must be the most beautiful mother in the world. And the most gracious, too—she seemed to know everyone's names as well as the names of their wives, husbands, and children. "How are you, dearest Eleni? How is your darling son Maximilian? Is he still riding and playing Kings? And how is your husband enjoying his work at the Ministry?" Ana couldn't imagine such clever words coming out of her own mouth.

The trill of a bamboo flute rose and hovered in the air as the shadow dancers wove through the crowd, leaping and turning. Ana's red velvet collar itched. She picked and scratched at it. She noticed a lot of people smiling at her, though, so she stopped what she was doing and dropped her hands to her sides.

The bamboo flute grew louder and more insistent. Just then Ana spotted her mother walking up to her, the green silk of her skirt swishing and crinkling around her ankles. There was a man at her side. He was dressed in gold and black, the royal colors of Kieska.

"Darling!" The queen enfolded Ana in her arms, too tightly. Ana flinched.

"Ana, I would like you to meet Ambassador Bertl," the queen announced loudly. "Bertl, this is my daughter, Tatiana Anatolia."

Ana found herself staring at the man. He had long, curly brown hair and lovely green eyes.

"Your Excellency," Bertl murmured, bowing. Then he took Ana's hand and kissed it.

Ana's cheeks burned. She gave a little cough. "Thank you for being here," she heard herself saying mechanically. Her mother had instructed her to say that to each and every guest. "I hope you are enjoying yourself."

"Yes, yes, of course."

"Bertl, have you tried the turtle's egg canapés?" the queen trilled.

Bertl didn't respond. Ana realized, with surprise, that he was looking at her—*her.* He seemed to be studying her as though she were a particularly fascinating plant.

"Veda, you have done well," Bertl said, finally.

"What do you mean, dear Bertl?"

"This. Your daughter. Look at her!" Bertl smiled at Ana in a way that made her blush even more deeply. "Your daughter, your little Tatiana, is going to be the greatest beauty in Ran someday. Take my word for it."

Ana's breath caught in her throat. No one had ever

said such words about her before. Her—a beauty? With her skinny limbs and wild hair and skinned knees? She found herself smoothing her red velvet skirt and wondering if her collar was straight.

"Bertl, you are always so perfectly charming," the queen said, tucking her arm through his. "Now, I must introduce you to my Minister of Education. . . ."

"Have you begun thinking about a husband for her?" Bertl asked the queen as she led him away. "I imagine that every prince alive will be fighting and clawing each other for the privilege. . . ."

As they walked off, Queen Veda cast a glance over her shoulder at Ana. Ana saw something in her eyes that she had never seen before.

It was fury, hatred.

The snow had stopped. Outside, the darkness was the uncertain color of the sea: here blue, here brown, here gray, here black. If there were stars or planets or moons to be seen, they were lost in the vague, disquieting palette of the night.

Ana sat at her dressing table, playing Science with her jars of unused creams and potions. She poured various scented oils—ambergris, jasmine, lily of the valley—into the jars, along with dirt and lead shavings and pieces of her shorn hair. The oils smelled heavy and sweet, and mingled in a fascinating way with the smells that clung to her from dinner: onion and meat tarts, garlic soup, pastries. On an impulse, Ana dipped her finger into one of the jars and smeared the mixture across her cheeks. War paint.

The door opened, and Omi rushed in.

"Could you not have knocked?" Ana said irritably.

Omi headed straight for Ana's closet and began rummaging through it. "Her Majesty wishes to see you right away."

"What?" Ana said, uncomprehending. Her mother almost never asked to see her.

"You must wear one of your lovely silk dresses. I will brush your hair. Where is your hairbrush? *What have you done to your hair?*" Omi cried out, suddenly noticing.

Ana gazed into the mirror and touched her head. "What do you mean? What's wrong with my hair?" she said innocently.

Omi muttered something Ana couldn't hear. She began digging through her pockets. "Perhaps with some hairpins and silk ribbons . . ."

"No, no ribbons! I'm fine. I can get ready by myself," Ana insisted.

"And what is that mess on your face?"

"It's nothing."

"But—"

❖

"It's nothing! Just leave me, I order you!"

Omi's face flushed bright red. Then she turned on her heels and walked out of the room. Ana felt the vaguest twinge of regret as she watched Omi go. She had not been very nice to her today.

"May the pink angels visit your dreams!" Ana called out after her. It was something they used to say to each other, before bedtime, in the old days.

There was no answer.

Ana sighed and turned back to the mirror. She would make it up to Omi later. For now, she had to get ready for her meeting with her mother.

A meeting with her mother. What did the queen want with her? Ana rarely saw her anymore. Not at meals, not after school, not any time at all. Ana had told herself that there must a reason for this. Perhaps her mother had a political crisis on her hands. Or perhaps she had been especially busy with her day-to-day duties lately.

Or perhaps Ana had done something wrong, and she was being punished. What could it be? Had she not gained enough weight? Had she inadvertently worn a pretty dress?

Ana gazed at herself in the mirror. She made herself smile, then frown, then smile again. A pretty smile, not one of those fake, insincere smiles, she could hear her mother saying.

Then she leaned closer to the mirror and tried to imagine—really imagine—what her mother would see. Pasty, dirty skin. Pimples and boils. Ragged, oily strands of hair. And of course there was the plain olive dress she had borrowed from one of the servant girls. It was a size too small for her, emphasizing the rolls of flesh.

Still, there were the eyes. They were her mother's eyes, enormous and deep and brown, with flecks of gold and amber. Nothing she did to herself seemed to affect their startling beauty.

What had she looked like, before? Ana could almost recall her long brown hair, how it shone like silk after Omi's brushings; her ivory skin; her radiant smile.

Then the pink angels had abandoned Ana's dreams.

But there had been no other way—no other choice, really. It had been clear to Ana since her twelfth birthday, since the incident with Ambassador Bertl, that her mother's love came with an unspoken condition. Simply, her mother could not bear to have Ana be more beautiful than she. And so, over time, Ana had made herself as unbeautiful as possible. Now her mother had no reason not to love her.

But Ana still craved—*craved*—more of her mother's affection. She would have to figure out how to get it, even if meant doubling her pastry consumption or cutting all her hair off. She would do whatever it took.

Ana picked up her skirts and hurried out the door. The halls, lit by torchlight, looked darkly ominous. The smell of boiled milk wafted up from the kitchen. One of the servant men hurried by, bowing deeply and murmuring "Your Ex'lency" as he passed Ana. Ana ignored him.

The queen's chambers were in the east wing of the castle, far from Ana's. Ana knocked on the gold-gilded double doors.

"It's me, Momi," Ana said in a loud voice. There was no reply.

Ana opened the doors a crack and entered, ever so quietly. Flute music was playing. The air was thick with lavender and eucalyptus. Flames curled and hissed in the massive stone fireplace, bathing the room in a hazy glow.

The queen was lying on her large canopied bed, facedown, naked. She was covered in layers and layers of gossamer white sheets. Two men, the twins named Brun and Balto, were giving her a massage.

The Beauty Consultant sat on a stool in the far corner of the room. He was turning the pages of a large yellowed book and muttering quietly to himself.

"Tatiana Anatolia," the queen murmured. She didn't look up or even open her eyes. "You've come to see your poor mother."

"Momi." Ana rushed across the room, knelt down by

the bed, and kissed one of her mother's dangling hands. Her lips grew slick with oil; the lavender and eucalyptus tasted strange and bitter. "Are you well? You're not ill, are you?"

"I am very tired, little one. Your mother is tired. It has been a long day. Harder, Brun, you are like an old woman tonight!"

"Beg pardon, Your Majesty."

Queen Veda sighed as Brun leaned his hefty weight into her shoulder blades, pressing and kneading. "Better, much better. Ana, darling, I just wanted a visit with you. Isn't a poor old mother entitled to a visit with her daughter? What are you studying in school these days?"

"History. And Numbers. Oh, and Astronomy, too, and Composition," Ana rattled off.

"And what do you compose?"

"Songs and poems, mostly."

"Sing me something you wrote, then."

Ana flushed with pleasure. It had been a long time since her mother had asked for a song from her. "Are you sure, Momi? I am not very good."

"Of course you are. You have always been my talented little songbird. Sing for me!" The queen turned her head so that Ana could no longer see her face.

"Yes. All right, then."

Ana sat up straight and cleared her throat. She considered various songs she could sing and dismissed them: too common, too stupid, too sad.

An ember crackled in the fireplace. Brun's and Balto's hands glided down the queen's back in perfect choreographed unison. Ana was vaguely aware of the Beauty Consultant staring at her from beneath his hooded eyes.

Ana took a deep breath and began singing to the back of her mother's head, to the tangled nest of glistening black curls:

There was a girl who wanted to be the wind
And travel across the sea to a distant land
And whistle through the grasses of the marsh
And topple fairy castles made of sand

The black curls rustled. Queen Veda turned her head, opened her eyes, and gazed sleepily at Ana. Her lips twisted into a smile. "Your hair."

Ana stopped singing. Her hands flew up to her head. "I . . . that is . . . I cut it today," she stammered. "I know I didn't do a very good job, Momi. I'm sorry if it displeases you."

"Oh, no, it's lovely. It's perfect. You are my pretty little girl, aren't you? My only child."

Ana blushed. "Yes, Momi."

"I will brush it for you. In a minute. As soon as these gentlemen are finished."

Queen Veda continued gazing at Ana, at her jagged, unruly hair and pocked skin and too-tight olive dress. The twins covered the queen's slick, shining back with a sheet and began working on her long, slender legs. Ana knew, in this moment, that her mother cared about her after all. She could see it in her face, in the expression of radiant pleasure that glowed like firelight in her eyes. Overcome with emotion, Ana reached forward and grasped one of her mother's hands.

Queen Veda pressed back, her nails digging slightly into Ana's flesh. Then she pulled away and rolled onto her back.

"The other side," she called out, and closed her eyes.

4

"I AM WARNING YOU, YOUR MAJESTY," SAID THE BEAUTY Consultant.

Queen Veda lay back against her pillows, entranced with the dewy glow of her skin. The boys had done a good job on her tonight. "What? What are you talking about?" she murmured. "Pass me my hand mirror, will you?"

The Beauty Consultant's eyes turned yellow with annoyance. "You are not listening! There will come a day when she will surpass you. You need to prepare yourself."

Queen Veda laughed.

"I need to prepare myself for nothing," she snapped. "You have seen her."

"She is your daughter," the Beauty Consultant replied. "She is your blood."

"Please. I have more important things to think about.

The list, for example. I want you to help me with the list."

The Beauty Consultant sighed. "Why do you seek my help with the list, when you do not care to listen to me about this other matter?"

The queen felt heat rise to her cheeks. She sat up, fists clenched, and had to resist the impulse to hit the small, shriveled, ugly little man for daring to cross her like this.

But she could not. The Lady Despina had been very clear. *You will not always like his counsel,* she had told her many years ago. *In fact, you will almost never like his counsel. But you must pay heed to his words. And you must never, ever make him angry.*

Queen Veda unclenched her fists. She tried to remember her breathing. *In four, hold four, out four, hold four . . .* She reached over to the cat, the long-haired silver one with the pointy ears, and stroked it.

It hissed and scrambled away. *Time for a new one,* the queen thought.

"I will consider what you have said about the other matter," she forced herself to say, finally, to the Beauty Consultant. "In the meantime I would appreciate your help on the list. Tomorrow morning, perhaps, after I exercise Dendril."

"Very good, Your Majesty."

She could only look into his eyes for a second

before turning away. They were a color she had never seen before, a color she could not even describe: blue, gray, brown, black, all swirling together in a maelstrom of—*something*. Premonition, maybe. The little man knew too much.

"You may go now," she said, sinking back into her pillows.

But he was already gone.

5

❧

"TODAY WE SHALL REVIEW HISTORY. WHO CAN TELL ME when the kingdom of Ran was founded?" Madame Winks peered around the room over her thick black spectacles.

A hand shot up in the air. It was Pell Fortunas again. Pell had given the last three answers while the rest of the class sat gazing with great intensity at their desktops, their scribe books, their hands.

Madame Winks did not feel like working to draw these other students out, however. For one thing, her compensation as a teacher was too insultingly paltry. The Ministry of Education did not seem to care enough about education to pay its teachers a decent salary. And for another thing, Madame Winks had imbibed too much chrysanthemum mead last night, and her head felt like a ball of hot, melting wax.

She touched her temples with her fingertips. "Yes, Pell?"

Pell sat up straight and smiled. Her cheeks were very round and pink, with soft, deep dimples. "In the Time of the Solstice, Year One. King Galen came and conquered the thirteen Patim warlords who had taken over our land. His rule began a golden time in our history. When he died, in Year Seven, Her Majesty Queen Veda took over. His wife," she added quickly, casting a sideways glance at Ana.

Ana caught Pell's glance. Pell's hand fluttered in an imperceptible wave.

"Very good, Pell," Madame Winks said. "Can someone tell me what reforms King Galen made during his six years of rule? Someone besides Pell and, of course, Her Excellency."

A few heads turned in Ana's direction. Ana slunk down in her chair and averted her eyes. She knew that most of the students considered her a freakish oddity, and not just because of her appearance. She, a princess, was attending the village school instead of receiving private tutoring.

Queen Veda had once explained to Ana that it was good for the royal family to "mix with the commoners." But as far as Ana could tell, her mother never bothered to mix with anyone except the nasty little man—and the twins Brun and Balto, and her other men friends.

Korb, a boy with a thick mop of black hair, attempted to answer. Ana half-listened to his memorized gleanings about King Galen's accomplishments—the improved army, the new water system, the programs to help the poor and ailing.

But Ana remembered little of Galen the king, only Galen the father. She remembered the smoky smell of his skin and his long curly hair that was the color of copper coins. She remembered their walks through the ancient redwood forest, their talks about everything. He had talked to her about farming, about medicine, about politics. He had talked to her about music and art. He had talked to her about courage and morality. He had talked to her about sacrifice.

He had been preparing her to lead the kingdom of Ran someday.

The tolling of the village bell interrupted the student Korb's recitation. There was a loud scraping of chairs and the sudden eruption of chatter.

"More History tomorrow!" Madame Winks said, cupping her hands around her mouth. "Please do your reading! And Toma, please try to be on time from now on!"

"Yes'm."

Ana stood up and slung her leather satchel over her

shoulder. She walked over to Pell, who was talking to three other girls. The girls glanced at Ana, curtsied, and hurried away. Most of the students at the school seemed uncomfortable around Ana. In truth, Pell was her only friend.

"Hello, Tati," Pell said, beaming with pleasure. Tati was Pell's special nickname for her.

"Pella Bella." Ana smiled. "Do you want to eat together?"

"A picnic," Pell agreed. "Momi baked this morning. She packed me some of her special chrysanthemum bread."

Ana wove her arm through Pell's. "Let's go, then."

Students were pouring into the village square, carrying their meals. It was a warm day; the snow had melted, and the ground was damp and green in anticipation of the new season.

Ana and Pell crossed the square, to the cobblestone path that led to the Enchanted Pond. As they moved through the crowd Ana noticed that most of the boys stared at Pell. Pell was beautiful, beyond beautiful, with her long blond hair, round pink cheeks, and lovely red dress that had been made by her grandmomi. None of the boys stared at Ana.

The girls soon reached the pond. It was entirely deserted except for a family of black swans grazing on weeds.

Ana spread her shawl down on the damp grass, and they sat down. "So," she said. "How is your family?"

"You mean, how is Stefan?" Pell replied, grinning. Ana blushed.

"Stefan is doing fine." Pell reached into her satchel for a bundle wrapped in blue cloth. "He is in his first year at the military academy. Momi says he will make a fine soldier. Or perhaps a royal guard at the palace."

"Well, she must be proud of him, then," Ana said, biting into one of her cloudberry pastries.

"That boy Korb asked me to go to the village fair with him," Pell said suddenly.

Ana giggled. "Will you go with him, then?"

Pell shrugged and bit into a piece of bread. "I don't know. I rather like Michaelas instead. Do you know that he can name all the moons in the far galaxies?"

"He must be very smart, then."

"He is! And I like his eyes."

Ana giggled again. When she and Pell were twelve, they had written down a list of all the boys at the school so they could consider which ones they might marry someday. They had chosen Liat for his fine looks and Alexandros for his swordsmanship and Darias for his funny stories. But in the end, they had decided that none of them were worthy of marriage.

Ana wasn't even sure she would be allowed to choose whom to marry. Her mother, a princess from

Kieska, had been chosen for Galen by her family elders. There were no family elders left in Ran anymore—just Queen Veda. No doubt she would want to select an appropriate mate for Ana.

One of the black swans ambled by. Ana tore a corner of her pastry and offered it. The swan ripped it out of her hand.

Of course, what man would have me like this? Ana thought.

"Tati." Ana glanced up and realized that Pell was staring at her. "Are you all right?"

"Mmm-hmm."

"No, I mean it. Truly. Are you all right?"

Ana stopped chewing. She brushed the crumbs off her brown wool skirt. "I'm okay."

"Are you . . . *sick*?" Pell said the last word in a whisper.

Ana shook her head. "I'm not sick."

"What is it, then?"

"It's nothing."

Pell frowned and looked away. More black swans ambled in their direction, smelling food. Ana hated lying to her best friend, but she didn't know what else to do. How could she explain what was happening? That there was a good reason she had allowed herself to become ugly? That she, Tatiana Anatolia, was not crazy?

But maybe she was. Her father had told her once,

during one of their long talks, about people who went mad. He had told her that the mind could become poisoned by disease, by obsession, by ancient corruptions of the blood, and thereby lose its fragile hold on reality.

Had her mind been poisoned by her love for her mother? Was the inside of her as sick as the outside? Sometimes, she felt as though she was making a horrible mistake—that she was destroying her flesh, her face, her beauty in order to attain something that was unattainable anyway.

Pella Bella, she wanted to say. *Help me.* But instead she turned away and bit down on her lip, hard, till she tasted blood. She did not want Pell to see the tears in her eyes.

6

ᚱ

ANA HAD MET PELL AT THE ENCHANTED POND NEARLY
ten years ago.

The pond was called that, or so the legend went,
because of a midwife named Saskia. Saskia had drowned
herself in the pond one brown, muddy day for reasons
having to do with her health or her state of mind, or perhaps a man she loved. People believed that when Saskia
sank and disappeared into the pond, its murky waters
had assumed her magic. And so the name.

Young Ana was swimming in the Enchanted Pond
one day, alone and without permission, when she
caught sight of a skinny blond girl hiding in a honey-
blossom bush. She waved to the girl.

"Don't you want to come in and swim?"

"Aren't you afraid?" the girl replied, peering out of
the bushes.

"Of what?"

"Of the witch's bones."

Ana laughed. "There are no witch's bones in here. Only angelfish and water lilies."

"Are you sure?"

"Positive!"

They began swimming together nearly every day after that. Other days, when it was cold or rainy or otherwise unsuitable for swimming, they played in the halls of the palace or ran around in the conservatory, making wreaths out of the queen's special beauty herbs. Omi yelled at them often, threatening this punishment or that if they didn't behave. But she never followed through on her threats.

Those were some of the happiest days of Ana's life.

Then the happiness ended.

One morning, a servant who was out walking the dogs found King Galen's body in the garden. The king's lips were blue; his limbs were contorted in unnatural ways; his eyes were wide open and full of terror. How, how could Ana's brave father have been terrified of anything? The palace doctor had declared a rare virus to be the cause of the king's death. The same rare virus had befallen a servant girl at the palace, Jana, just weeks before.

Grief, Ana discovered, was like the thing she had felt when she broke her leg as a little girl. It was a searing pain that flooded her entire body and made her want to die. Except this pain permeated not just her body but her heart, her soul, her brain, her every waking thought.

Omi had been away visiting her sister in Catonia, so Pell was Ana's only comfort during that time. At the king's funeral Pell snuck past the royal guards to sit at Ana's feet and offer her small gifts out of her skirt pockets: a ragged ribbon, a tortoiseshell comb, pieces of milk candy. She hugged Ana's knees as Ana wept, which she did very quietly so as not to disturb the queen. The queen sat through the entire ceremony in stony silence, her exquisite face covered with a black lace veil, and did not glance at Ana once except to issue a whispered warning: "Get hold of yourself, Tatiana Anatolia."

When Pell's own father died in a mining accident the following year, leaving the Fortunas family almost penniless, Ana begged her mother to send them money each full moon until the youngest boy, Milo, was old enough to work. Much to Ana's surprise, the queen granted her wish.

To this day, Pell's mother sent gifts to the palace almost daily: baskets of chrysanthemum bread, sweet goat butter, beautiful blankets made of lamb's wool. And Pell mentioned the queen in every prayer. She didn't seem to mind that the queen never remembered her name.

Although, one day the queen had summoned Ana to her room and asked, "Who is that blond girl from your school? The one you play with?" When Ana had answered, "Pell Fortunas," the Beauty Consultant had written Pell's name down in a purple notebook. For the briefest moment Ana had imagined that her mother was planning a birthday party for her—the first in four years. A party—for *her*? Ana had immediately felt ashamed for even thinking of it.

7

$\maltese$

SOON AFTER THE DAY AT THE POND, ANA HAD A DREAM.

In the dream she was walking through a cave made of ice and diamonds. Her father was at her side, dressed in bearskin. She was dressed in a long, hooded coat made of white fur. Three white rabbits ran alongside them.

A strange wind blew through the cave, whistling through Ana's hair, chilling her even through her heavy clothing. Icicles tingled like chimes. Diamonds sparkled and shimmered in the lamplight.

Ana tried to speak. But her father silenced her. "This is a holy place," he whispered. "You must not say anything until we reach the end."

The end of what? Ana wanted to ask him. *What is this cave? And why is it holy?*

Just then the three white rabbits came to a halt and

began screaming. It was a terrible sound—the sound of dying.

"Popi!" she cried out. "What's wrong with the rabbits?"

"Stay here," her father ordered her.

Then he was gone—vanished. She was alone with the screaming rabbits.

"Popi, what do I do?" she shouted.

The rabbits continued screaming.

Ana was awakened by the soft *plink* of something hitting her window. Where were the screaming rabbits? Where was her father? Her sheets were drenched, and her hair clung to her face in sweaty tatters. It took her a long moment to understand that she had been dreaming.

Slowly she opened her eyes and blinked into the darkness. No rabbits. No Galen. Instead, at the foot of her bed were two puddles of black fur: Jewel and Jax. She had found the cats abandoned, nearly dead, in the schoolyard many years ago. Across the room a tall, drooping candle flickered and threatened to go out.

There was another *plink*. Ana sat up and gathered a blanket around her shoulders, making the two cats meow in protest. She realized that someone was outside, trying to get her attention. Who could it be, at this late hour? What if the noise woke the queen? She rose from her bed and tiptoed to the window. She opened the shutters, shivering when the cold night air hit her face.

Pell was standing below, in the garden. She wore a heavy black cloak over her white nightgown and thick, crusty-looking leather boots. She waved furiously when she saw Ana.

"Pell! What are you doing?" Ana called out in alarm.

"Come down, Ana. I have news!"

"You're crazy!"

"Come down!"

"All right!"

Grabbing a shawl and a candle, Ana hurried out of her room and down the stairs. There were no servants or guards in the hallways except the cook's assistant Melk, curled up on a stone bench and sleeping off his mead. Melk's very fat dog, Bones, was curled up on the floor, gasping and snoring.

Ana soon reached the kitchen. Everything was silent; copper pots and pans gleamed on their hooks; a mangy yellow cat scurried under a cupboard. Ana unlatched the back door and opened it.

"Tati!" Pell was standing there, trembling in the cold.

"Pella, get in here!"

Pell rushed inside, grabbed Ana, and hugged her. Ana felt dizzy from the unexpected intensity of the embrace, the frigid air mingling with the warmth of the kitchen. The coarse wool of Pell's cloak scratched her skin.

Ana broke away and stared into Pell's eyes. "Pella, what is it? What's happened?"

Pell smiled radiantly. "Oh, Tati!"

"Did Michaelas ask you to the village fair?"

Pell broke into a loud peal of laughter. "No, nothing like that. Michaelas is irrelevant now. Look at what Momi received today!" She reached into the pocket of her cloak and handed Ana a crinkled envelope.

Ana took the envelope and held it closer to the candlelight. She stifled a gasp when she recognized the bloodred seal. It was the royal seal of Ran. Her mother's seal.

"Go ahead, open it!" Pell urged her.

Ana opened the envelope and shook out the letter. She couldn't imagine why her mother would be writing to Pell's mother, unless it had something to do with the allowance. Perhaps the queen had increased it to a more sizeable amount?

Ana unfolded the pale dove-colored stationery and began to read.

Dear Madame Fortunas, it began. The spidery handwriting was not the queen's. *It is with great pleasure that I inform you that your daughter, Pell, has been selected to attend a new school for young women. The Academy is an elite institution which will host no more than fifty young women from Ran who possess exceptional personal and academic potential. Your daughter will be living and studying there beginning with the first day of the new season. . . .*

Ana stopped reading. Her thoughts were swirling. What was this "Academy"? Why had the queen never mentioned it to her?

And then it occurred to her. Perhaps the queen was not going to send her there. Perhaps she wished for Ana to continue to "mix with the commoners." Or perhaps she did not think Ana was worthy of this new school. Ana's heart clenched up like a fist.

"Well?" Pell demanded.

"I—I don't know what to say," Ana murmured. "Congratulations, I guess."

"You guess? You *guess*? Tati, this is the greatest honor of my life!" Pell scolded. "Momi told me the news after dinner. I couldn't wait to tell you. That's why I snuck out after everyone went to bed!"

"Oh, Pell." Ana reached over and hugged her. "Congratulations. I'm very happy for you. It's just that—well, where *is* this Academy, anyway?"

"In the mountains, you silly Tati," Pell giggled. Then she frowned. "You really didn't know? But . . . your mother didn't tell you?"

Ana shook her head.

"But aren't you going to the Academy too?" Pell asked her. "I thought for sure that you would be going too."

"I don't think so," Ana shrugged. "I mean, Momi hasn't mentioned it."

"Oh!"

Pell began pacing around the kitchen. The mangy yellow cat emerged from under the cupboard and scurried across the floor, zigzagging to avoid Pell's feet.

"But you *have* to go! How can I go there without you?" Pell said finally.

"I will ask her tomorrow," Ana said. "Maybe she meant to tell me in person."

Pell smiled hopefully. "Yes, yes! That must be it!"

"You should get back before your momi misses you."

"You're right."

Pell took the letter from Ana and carefully folded it. Then she gave Ana one last hug. "Let's meet at the pond tomorrow morning," she said.

"Yes, tomorrow."

After Pell left, Ana walked over to the cupboard and opened it. There was half a loaf of bread and a large hunk of orange cheese. The cheese had a fine layer of blue mold growing on it.

Ana took the bread and cheese and sat down on the cold stone floor. There, with the mangy cat hovering nearby, she began to tear at the hard bread and the moldy, distasteful cheese with her teeth. Crumbs spread across her lap. Mold clung to her lips.

The Academy. What was this Academy? And why had her mother never mentioned it to her?

8

"HAVE YOU HAD A CHANCE TO THINK ABOUT THE MATTER we discussed, Your Majesty?"

Queen Veda glanced up from her dressing table. The Beauty Consultant was standing in the doorway. Today he was dressed in a strange costume made of moss green velvet. He reminded her of an exotic medicine plant or a fungus.

"Oh, it's you," the queen replied brusquely.

She did not like being interrupted in the middle of her morning ablutions. For one thing, the daily ritual was long and difficult. First she washed her face in a porcelain bowl full of ice water, fresh mint leaves, and crushed rose petals. After that she caked on a thick mask made of clay from the Enchanted Pond. It was foul-smelling, like sulfur and rotting leaves, but she endured it because of its remarkable ability to make her look half her age.

She had the mask on her face now. She did not

particularly care to have the Beauty Consultant see her with a layer of oozing mud on her face. But he had left her little choice, entering her chambers at this ridiculously early hour without first clearing it with her.

"I said, have you had a chance to think about the matter we discussed?" the Beauty Consultant repeated, moving toward her.

"What matter?" she asked him idly. She turned in her seat and made herself look at him.

Beneath their hooded lids, his eyes glowed yellow. She frowned, wondering what was agitating him like this.

"*Serana du bis ferre,*" the Beauty Consultant muttered under his breath. "*Canna forbiere du mar.*"

"You know I cannot understand you when you use that, that *language,*" Queen Veda snapped. "What matter are you speaking of? Please be direct. I have a great deal on my mind, you know."

The Beauty Consultant continued muttering in his language for another moment. Then, abruptly, he switched to her tongue. "Your *daughter,*" he said, with emphasis. "She turns sixteen years in the new season. You must do something."

The queen sighed. Why was the tedious little man being so insistent about Ana? There was a time, perhaps, when Ana could have posed a serious threat to everything Veda had worked so hard to achieve. But that was no longer the case. Clearly Ana had plummeted into some vast pit of darkness from which there seemed to be no return.

Let the girl stuff herself with cloudberry pastries for all of eternity, she thought. Let her chop off her hair. Let her run around smelling like boiled onions. It made things so much easier.

"I still don't understand the case you are trying to make," she said to the Beauty Consultant. "Ana is not a problem."

"But she *could* be," the Beauty Consultant said. "She has your genetics. And"—he hesitated, but only for a second—"she has the benefit of true youth."

Queen Veda rose abruptly. Her velvet chair toppled to the floor. "How dare you!" she cried out.

The Beauty Consultant did not respond. He was staring at the queen's red silk robe, which had come undone. She realized then that she must look absurd— half naked, her face covered with mud, shouting. She didn't care if her servants saw her like this, or even Brun and Balto. But *he* was another matter.

With a small cough she bent down and restored the chair to its upright position. She closed her robe practically up to her neck. Then, sitting down, she took a moist honey-scented cloth and wiped the mud gently from her face.

The Beauty Consultant waited. The queen gave another small cough.

"Fine. Let us discuss this matter," she said at last.

"That is most advisable, Your Majesty."

"What do you think I should do?"

"I have a suggestion," the Beauty Consultant replied. His eyes turned from yellow to silver. "You must send her away."

"Send her away? Where?"

"The solution will come to you. In time."

The queen sighed with impatience. "No riddles, please. Tell me!"

The Beauty Consultant bowed. "That is all. I recommend that you devote your morning meditation to this problem."

With that, he left the room.

The queen bit back an angry retort. *Breathe,* she told herself. It would not be good to start her morning in such an unharmonious mood. It would show on her face and in her eyes, and undo all her hard work.

She turned in her seat. She lit a tall white candle, then stared at herself in the mirror.

Flawless ivory skin. Long black curls. Naturally red lips.

It is not possible, she thought.

But what if it is?

She continued staring at herself in the mirror, breathing deeply, and began meditating on the Beauty Consultant's words.

9

❧

Rain fell softly as Ana made her way through the garden. She could almost hear the leaves trembling under the weight of each drop, smell the long-dormant soil being awakened and upturned.

Changing, everything was changing. The new season was almost upon them now. And with it, Pell would be going away to her school, leaving Ana behind.

In the last several days Ana had learned of other girls whose families had received the letter. There were Eris and Hali from the village school. There were other girls from there too, whose names Ana did not know. Ana would see them gathering in the village square after their lessons were done, whispering and giggling.

They always tried to engage Pell in their conversations, mostly without success. Once, when Pell was forced to join them, she kept glancing over her shoulder at Ana with a worried expression.

The queen had not mentioned a word about the Academy to Ana. Clearly Ana was not going to be attending along with Pell and the other girls. She had told herself many stories about this, had invented many excuses for her mother's silence. Her mother did not want Ana to go so far away from her. Her mother was afraid of disappointing her.

Indeed, the Academy was far away, deep in the Horon mountains. And Pell and the others would be there for a long time. Pell had said something about being there for ten full moons before they would be permitted to come home to see their families. The program was particularly rigid, and the curriculum extremely demanding.

The rain was falling harder now. Ana hurried her steps until she reached the hut.

Rain poured off the steep copper roof as she stepped gingerly through the doorway, trying to avoid a mud puddle. Her clothes were drenched; her hair clung to her face in wet, sloppy tendrils. She shrugged off her cloak and threw it over a wooden crate.

"I'm here," she called out. "I'm sorry I kept you waiting."

The rabbits were in their separate cages, their bodies

folded into tight round shapes. It took a moment before they realized that Ana had arrived. Then they were up on their hind feet, or hopping around frantically, their pink noses twitching and trembling and pushing through the bars of their cages.

Ana laughed. "Oh! So you're hungry," she chided them.

She reached into her skirt pocket and pulled out a handful of greens. She had gotten them from the cook, who claimed that rabbits were only good for stew, but who nevertheless always seemed to have spare greens for Ana to take to the hut.

The rabbits made soft, eager clicking noises with their teeth. Ana walked over to the first cage and offered the rabbit—a big brown one she had named Bear—a leafy morsel. Bear tore the whole thing from her hands and retreated to the corner of his cage to devour it.

Ana moved on to the next cage, then the next. She saved her favorite rabbit—a small white one she had named Baby—for last.

"There you go," Ana whispered to Baby as she fed her. Baby never took the food from Ana outright, but insisted that she feed her, bite by bite. Ana knelt down on the hay-covered ground and pushed a leafy bit of green through the bars. Baby nibbled delicately at it.

After Baby was done, Ana opened the cage door and reached for her. Baby did not like to be held—none of the rabbits did—but for some reason, Ana was determined to teach Baby to enjoy the experience.

Ana stroked first Baby's nose, then the back of her neck. Baby gave a rabbit-purr of pleasure. Then, with a quick motion, Ana scooped up Baby with one hand and secured her hind legs with the other to keep her from kicking. Rabbits had fragile spines, Ana knew; if Baby kicked hard enough, she could break hers and die.

Baby squirmed and snorted in protest. Ana held Baby against her chest, against her pounding heart. "There, there," she cooed.

She could feel Baby's body trembling and heaving. She held her tighter and delivered tiny kisses to her head. The trembling and heaving eased slightly, then ceased. Stillness.

Ana smiled contentedly and closed her eyes. She had so much love to give, and she wanted—needed—for someone, something, to receive it. It was deeply satisfying to hold the small, soft rabbit in her arms.

Then Baby gave a sudden, swift kick with her hind legs and tried to scramble out of Ana's grip. Panicked, Ana grabbed the rabbit by her midsection and stuffed her back into her cage. Ana slammed the cage door shut. She was breathing hard. She realized that her hands were covered with deep red scratches.

"That was not very nice," Ana scolded Baby.

Baby hopped into her hay dish, curled up into a ball,

and stared at Ana with dark, furious eyes.

They are rabbits. You must learn to respect their nature, Omi had told her once.

But Ana didn't agree. Living things had their natures. But living things could also change.

Ana dipped her handkerchief in a bucket of rainwater and dabbed at her bloody scratches. "Tomorrow," she said to Baby. "Maybe tomorrow you'll let me hold you."

It was her mother who had taught Ana to love animals.

Once, when Ana was a young girl, she and the queen were taking a carriage ride through the mountains when they caught sight of a dead doe. There was an arrow stuck in its chest; it appeared as though a hunter had shot it but had been unable, or unwilling, to collect his trophy.

Unexpectedly the queen ordered the driver to stop the carriage. Scooping up her gray silk skirts, she descended to the damp, mossy ground and knelt beside the doe. And began to cry.

"Momi!"

Ana followed her mother and knelt by her side. Tears streamed down the queen's face, mingling with the black kohl that lined her eyes and the rose-pink powder that covered her cheeks.

"Momi, it's okay," Ana said, hugging her.

"It is not okay, Ana. Animals are innocent creatures. They don't deserve to die," the queen answered, weeping.

Before leaving, the queen ordered the driver to bury the deer so the boars would not find it and tear it apart. Then she picked a single mayapple blossom, laid it upon its grave, and prayed.

"May the gods watch over you always. May you rest in eternal sleep among the stars."

After that day, Ana noticed that whenever the queen saw a wild or stray animal, she would bow her head and say a quick prayer of protection for it under her breath. Ana began to do the same. She liked doing exactly as her mother did. She was also fascinated by the thought that somehow, in some mysterious way, her prayers could actually influence the fate of these creatures.

Many moons later Ana learned that the queen had ordered all the dogs on the castle grounds to be shot. Apparently a contagious disease, likely fatal, was sweeping through their population. Ana ran to her mother's room to plead with her to change her mind; was there no other option? No hope for a remedy? But the queen had been sedated by the royal doctor so as not to have to hear the gunshots. The suffering of the animals, the doctor informed Ana, was not even close to the suffering the queen felt in having had to make this difficult decision.

When the gunshots began, Ana knelt down on the cold floor of the castle hall and began to pray.

But her prayers did not work.

10

✥

THE RAIN HAD STOPPED. ANA CLOSED THE DOOR TO THE rabbit hut and started back for the castle.

The air was cool and damp, with a faint salty smell that reminded Ana of the sea. Her father used to take her to the sea, to teach her about sailing and tides and spotting enemy ships. Ana had a silvery-green shell from their last trip together; she had gone shelling when she was supposed to be practicing with her oars. Still, despite her tendency to such distractions, she had absorbed all of her father's lessons. She knew how to captain a schooner, predict when the tide was turning, and identify an unfamiliar fleet against the far horizon. Although she had no idea when she would ever use those skills now.

The light was growing dim. Soon it would be evening. Picking up her skirts, Ana ran back to the castle and up the main stairs to her room. She wanted to get out of her wet things. She also wanted to plan what pastries to eat for dinner, and how many. It wouldn't do for her to start growing thin.

Her mother was waiting for her in her room.

"Momi!" Ana rushed up to her mother, who was sitting at her dressing table. She knelt down by her side. "Is something wrong?"

The queen was wearing a pale blue dress with a simple white jewel at her throat. To Ana, she looked almost frail.

She had been studying one of Ana's Science jars. It was filled with lily of the valley cream, bits of her shorn hair, and a few dead, wingless flies. She set the jar down and cupped Ana's face in her hands. "You're cold! My poor bird, you've been walking in the rain."

"Yes, Momi. I was visiting with . . . that is, I was admiring the new flowers in the garden."

"You must get out of those clothes immediately, or you will become ill."

"Yes, Momi."

"Let me pick something out for you."

The queen got up and held on to the dressing table briefly, as if to steady herself. Walking over to Ana's closet, she began scanning the long row of dresses with her fingertips.

Ana got up too, and stood there. Speechless. She

watched her mother touch one dress, reject it, touch another. What was she doing here, in Ana's room? And why was she helping Ana get dressed? She had not helped Ana get dressed in many years—and even then, very rarely. It was always Omi's job.

"Here! This will be lovely on you."

The queen pulled out a plain green wool dress. Ana used to wear it long ago, before she had gotten so big. She doubted that she could fit into it any more.

"But Momi—" she began.

"Go ahead, Tatiana. I picked it out just for you."

Ana fell silent. It would be disrespectful of her to reject her mother's choice. And she couldn't afford to be even a *little* disrespectful, lest she shatter whatever spell had led her mother here, to her room, for a visit. The first in so long.

"Thank you, Momi," Ana said, taking the green dress from her.

The queen beamed. "Let me see you get into it!"

Ana blushed.

"It's only us girls, after all," the queen insisted.

There was no escaping it. Ana draped the green dress across the footboard of her bed and began unbuttoning.

Ana was aware of her mother watching her as she slipped off her dress. The dress was damp and wrinkled. Ana could smell Baby's fur on it. Now she was down to her white camisole and underskirt.

The queen regarded Ana. "Turn around, Tatiana Anatolia. I have not seen you in a long time."

Ana turned, slowly. She could feel her cheeks burning.

"You're a young woman now," the queen said. "Not my little girl anymore."

"I am not beautiful like you," Ana replied.

The queen smiled. "No, no, you're perfect! You are my angel!"

"I am?" Ana said. She felt a rush of pleasure at her mother's unexpected compliment.

"Besides, there is so much more to life than beauty," the queen went on. "Your studies, for example. You are a very smart girl. In fact, that is what I have come to talk to you about."

"My studies? What do you mean?"

"You may have heard people talking about the new school," her mother said. "The Academy. In the mountains. I would like for you to attend."

Ana's breath caught in her throat. "You want me to . . . attend the Academy?"

"Of course," her mother replied. "The royal family must be represented there. And it will be a wonderful experience for you. So much better than that simpleton village school."

"Oh!"

Somehow Ana found the edge of her bed and managed to sit down. She realized suddenly that she was chilled. She wrapped her arms around her chest. Jewel and Jax woke up from their naps and rubbed against her legs, purring.

This was what Ana had wanted so badly, to go to the Academy, to be with Pell. Yet, now that it was a reality, Ana felt an unexpected wave of despair wash over her. She wanted to be with Pell; yet how could she leave her mother? It was unthinkable.

"Dearest." The queen approached her and knelt down on the floor by Ana's side. The heady smell of her musky perfume filled the air between them. There was something else mixed in with it—the smell of strong wine. "You will learn a great deal at this school. It will prepare you to rule this kingdom someday."

"You mean, take your place?" Ana gasped. "No, no! I want you to be queen forever."

"Someday it will be your time. And you must be prepared. It is your duty."

Galen used to tell her this, and Ana had accepted his wishes—and his instructions—willingly. Of course it was her duty. Of course she had to be prepared. But these words, coming from her mother, only made her feel terror, despair. She couldn't imagine taking her mother's place.

✦

Ana bit her lip. "I don't want to leave you," she whispered.

"It will only be for a little while," the queen said. "Besides, you will be able to be with your friend—what is her name, Bell? Now, finish getting dressed so we can have our dinner. I asked the cook to set a table for us in the solarium so we can see the new baby swans."

"We're having dinner . . . together?"

"Yes, of course."

"Really?"

Ana stood up and began fussing busily with the buttons of her green dress. She turned her head so that her mother would not see the tears in her eyes. At this moment she wanted desperately to throw herself at her mother's feet, to laugh, to weep. But she did not want to spoil the moment or give her mother an opportunity to change her mind: *You are overreacting, Tatiana Anatolia; perhaps it is better that you eat alone.*

It had all been worth it: the looks at school, the horrible bloating of her belly, the pocks on her skin. The emptiness she felt every time she saw herself in the mirror. Her mother truly loved her—finally, again. And Ana would not risk losing that a second time.

11

✥

"IT IS DONE, THEN," QUEEN VEDA SAID. "I HAVE TAKEN your advice."

The Beauty Consultant did not reply. He was gazing intently at one of the new plants in the conservatory, a long, gnarled vine dotted with clusters of yellowish-green blossoms. A peculiar-looking red spider was crawling along the vine. The Beauty Consultant leaned closer and fixed his gaze on it. The spider slowed down, then stopped in its tracks.

The Beauty Consultant continued to stare at it. A few seconds later the spider fell to the ground. Dead.

"Can you please stop playing with your little bugs and pay attention to what I am saying?" the queen demanded. She swatted a hanging vine out of her face.

The Beauty Consultant picked up the spider with his

fingers. A thin stream of milky drool streamed down from its mouth. "This will make an excellent potion for your skin."

Queen Veda's hands flew up to her cheeks. "What? What is wrong with my skin?"

"With wild mushrooms and devil weed and rose petals. Ten of them, no more."

"What are you talking about?" she snapped. Only *he* could make her feel this way—a most unpleasant combination of anger and self-doubt.

"I will mix the potion for you. You will be pleased with it."

"Fine. But will you listen to me? I am sending Ana away. To the Academy."

The Beauty Consultant glanced up from his dead spider. His eyes glowed orange. "Very good, Your Majesty."

"She will be leaving with the others, at the next full moon."

"Yes, very good."

The Beauty Consultant slipped the dead spider into the pocket of his cloak and moved on to the next plant. It was a black, bell-shaped flower covered with tiny green specks. It emitted an oppressively sweet smell, like the smell of overripe fruit, of decay.

The queen realized suddenly that the tiny green specks were moving. The Beauty Consultant leaned toward the flower. His eyes burned dark orange, then red.

"What is it?" the queen asked him curiously.

The Beauty Consultant scraped the black flower with his finger, then licked his finger. "*Gomi,* just as I thought," he said delightedly.

"What?"

"*Gomi,* a very rare insect that feeds only on this particular flower," the Beauty Consultant replied.

"Oh. I see."

"One must carefully study the relationship between flowers and insects," he went on. "Some insects help the growth of their partner flowers. Some do the opposite and destroy them. Either way, these insects are a valuable ingredient in beauty formulas. They take in the cosmetic properties of the flowers by eating them, and then enhance them with their own digestive juices and other biochemical processes. Furthermore . . ."

The little man's words were making the queen dizzy. Usually he didn't talk quite so much. She turned away from him, from the bright midday sun that was blazing like fire through the glass walls of the conservatory. She took a few steps toward the shade of a sprawling blue tree that grew in the corner.

Its branches hung heavy with some unrecognizable fruit. Queen Veda ripped off one of its wide blue leaves and began fanning herself with it.

Just then a small worm dropped from the leaf and onto her chest. It had a silvery body and a purplish, gaping mouth. It coiled into a circle, then uncoiled again.

The queen tried to brush it off, but it clung stubbornly to her skin. "Get this thing off of me!" she ordered the Beauty Consultant.

"That is a rare type of *biala* worm," he observed with interest. He reached up, plucked it off the queen's chest, and stuffed it into his cloak pocket. "A mere infant. Excellent for a formula that brightens the eyes. Unfortunately it can be extremely deadly. If it had bitten you, you would be dead by nightfall. Perhaps sooner."

The queen felt her blood turn cold. "I would be . . . dead? That thing is poisonous?"

"Very."

"Could you not have warned me?"

But the Beauty Consultant ignored her outburst. "I will make the formula for you," he said. "One *biala* worm with its mouth removed, celandine, lady's mantle, and two vials of hazel water, no more."

"Fine. In fact, have it ready by dinnertime. I have a guest."

"Very good, Your Majesty."

"And in the future, I do not wish to hold our meetings in this place. Is that understood?"

"Very good, Your Majesty."

Beauty

The queen made herself take a deep breath. She used to love the conservatory with its lush universe of greenery, herbs, and wild, exotic blossoms even in the dead of winter. It had always been calming—comforting, even.

But no more. Ever since the Beauty Consultant had started growing his bizarre medicinal plants, experimenting with crossbreeding and hydroponics, and encouraging rare insect species to live in the environment, the place had become freakish, hostile. She felt as though her skin were crawling with tiny green specks, silver worms, spiders; she couldn't move without getting caught in some carnivorous-seeming vine. She was anxious to get back to her room and take a long, cleansing bath.

"Would you like the skin formula by dinnertime as well, Your Majesty?"

"Yes, yes. Just take care of it."

Of course there was a time when her beauty did not require such intervention and effort. When she first met Galen, she was only slightly older than Ana. Galen had taken one look at her perfect face, her black curls cascading down her back, her slender young girl's body sheathed in pink lace—and he had fallen to his knees and begged her father, King Ramos, for her hand in marriage. Galen seemed to have forgotten that the matter had already been settled; her parents had arranged the union with his parents over many goblets of mead at a private meeting in the mountains.

The wedding had been lavish, lasting six days. She had wanted it to be formal, intimate, with only royalty and heads of territories. But her father, who played so well at magnanimity, had invited the entire village. And so every farmer, every silversmith, every ditch digger in Kieska had shown up. They had shown up in their shabby cloaks and tunics and dresses, wearing meticulously polished boots that nevertheless tracked mud across the marble floors.

There were endless dances, endless speeches, endless feasts: whole boars, roasted rabbits, platters piled high with fruit that had been brought in from the far islands. Galen had not taken his eyes off her, not once, not even when he was supposed to be forging alliances and discussing treaties.

Mischa, too, had not taken his eyes off her. Neither had Kyros. If either man begrudged that he was not the groom, it was not obvious. Mischa, however, had caught her in an unguarded moment in the courtyard; she had gone out there to escape the crowd, to collect her thoughts, to enjoy a glass of wine alone. And on the last night of the festivities, Kyros had followed her to her chambers when she had gone there to change from her day clothes into her evening clothes.

What was she to do? She had loved these men, once.

Later, when she found out that Mischa had died under suspicious circumstances during a hunting trip and that Kyros had committed suicide by poison the same day, she locked herself in her room and wept for many hours. But by dinnertime, as Galen sat across the table from her, drinking many bottles of mead in stony silence and looking up only to say "No more," she managed to smile innocently and say, "Whatever you wish, my lord."

That was in the beginning.

Many years later, after Ana was born, Veda started noticing the changes: the sagging of her belly and breasts, the wrinkles fanning out from the corners of her eyes, the brown spots on her once-spotless skin. That Ana grew more beautiful every day as Veda grew less beautiful only compounded the aggravation, the sheer tragedy, of the situation.

And then, when Galen stopped spending his nights in her chambers, and she saw him conversing with the red-haired servant girl once too often, she realized that something had to be done.

Unfortunately the problem didn't end there.

12

OMI PUT THE LAST OF ANA'S DRESSES INTO A TRUNK.

"The cold-weather things are on the bottom. The velvet things, the wool things. Your cloaks and shawls," Omi explained. "The warm-weather things are on top. You will have a uniform to wear at the school."

Ana scraped a fingernail across her bare arm. It left a satisfying wake of dead, white, flaky skin.

"What uniform?"

"I don't know. A simple dress, I would imagine."

The flakes of skin fluttered onto the dressing table. Ana pushed them into a tiny pile.

"How many girls will be there?"

"Your mother said around fifty. From all the villages in Ran."

"Who will our teachers be?"

Beauty

❖❖❖

"I don't know, Ana. I'm sure they will be very fine teachers. This is a very special school, after all."

Ana flicked the pile of dead skin with her fingertip. It looked like ashes against the dark wooden surface of the table. She thought about her mother's smooth, white, perfect skin—and Pell's, too—which no doubt resulted from daily bathing, scrubbing, and the application of fine emollients. For a fleeting moment Ana felt a pang of loneliness. Her mother and Pell shared a beauty ritual with each other and with other women which she did not share. She was a freak, an outsider. Although this was nothing new.

"Why is the school only for girls?" she asked Omi.

Omi sighed. "I don't know, child. You are filled with questions today! Come, you must get dressed now. The carriage will be leaving shortly."

"Fine, all right."

Ana got up from her dressing table and walked over to her closet. Without thinking, she pulled a blue-gray dress off its hook and slipped it on over her undergarments. The dress was loose, flowing, with cream-colored lace trim along the sleeves. Ana touched the lace. It was so pale, so delicate, with an intricate pattern of rosebuds.

Ana used to love lace. She used to love this dress, in fact. It was one of the prettiest ones she owned, and she had not worn it in a very long time.

Then it occurred to her that she should take it off

and put on something else—something less becoming. What if her mother should see her in it? It might upset her and make her think Ana was being disobedient.

But I'm going away, she told herself. *I'm going away, and she will only see me for a minute anyway. If that.*

"Ana! You look beautiful in that dress!"

Ana glanced up and realized that Omi was beaming at her from across the room.

"No, I don't," Ana protested. She began to take the dress off.

"Stop it! You look lovely! And besides, we have no time for this."

"Oh, all right."

Ana tugged the garment back on. The small sliver of pleasure she had felt about the dress, about the lace, was gone. She slipped a pair of black boots over her heavy gray stockings. She ran her fingers through her hair, which was greasy from days of not washing. Or had it been weeks?

"I am very proud of you, do you know that, Ana?" Omi told her. She folded Ana's soft pink blanket, the one she'd slept with for years, and placed it carefully in the trunk. Then she closed the trunk and locked it. "Everyone is. Your mother, especially."

Ana looked up. "She is? How do you know?"

"Why, I just know. She told me how pleased she was about your going to this new school."

Hope stirred in Ana's chest. "Will she be seeing me off?"

Omi hesitated. "I'm sure she will try to. Although of course she's always liable to be called away on some business or the other. Come on, child, let's stop our dawdling and go downstairs."

"One second!"

Ana rushed to her bed and kissed Jax and Jewel, who were sleeping together like two curved spoons. "Be good, you tiny darlings," she murmured at their warm, furry heads. "Listen to Omi and don't give her any trouble. I'll see you very, very soon."

"I'll take good care of them, Ana. Don't you worry," Omi promised her.

"And the rabbits, too?"

"And the rabbits, too."

"Jax loves meat. Jewel can't eat any meat whatsoever, it makes her ill. Baby—that's the little white rabbit—needs to be fed by hand. Every day. Just don't try to pick her up, or any of the other rabbits either!"

"I know, I know."

Tears stung Ana's eyes as she regarded her cats, her room, the view out her window one last time. Was she doing the right thing? Should she refuse to go to the Academy and stay with her cats, her rabbits, Omi—and most importantly, her mother?

But the queen had been clear. Ana was to go.

"Come on, child," Omi said gently.

"Yes. Okay."

Ana brushed her tears aside. Then she allowed Omi to lead her downstairs as two servant boys followed, carrying her trunk.

A black carriage was waiting in the courtyard, tied to two large chestnut horses. The driver, a short, silver-haired man whom Ana did not recognize, tipped his hat at her.

"G'morning, Your Excellency."

Ana looked around the courtyard. "Where is my mother?" she asked him.

"Not seen her yet this morning, Your Excellency."

"Oh."

"A fine day for a drive through the mountains, Your Excellency."

"Yes, yes."

Ana took a deep breath, trying not to worry. Was her mother not going to see her off, after all? Maybe she had found out that Ana was wearing the pretty blue-gray dress and decided not to come down, as a demonstration of her displeasure.

Ana turned to Omi. "I must go up to her room and say good-bye to her!"

"I don't know if that is a good idea, Ana—," Omi began.

But Omi's voice was drowned out by the thunder of

hoofbeats. Queen Veda, sitting high on her favorite mount Dendril, appeared suddenly in the courtyard. Behind her was a man on a gray stallion. He had long, golden-blond hair and wore a military uniform.

"Tatiana Anatolia!"

The queen brought Dendril to a full stop and dismounted quickly, gracefully. Ana ran up to her and threw her arms around her.

"Momi! I thought you weren't coming!"

The queen tossed her head and laughed. "Of course I was coming, my angel. I wouldn't miss saying goodbye to you for anything!"

"Oh, I am so glad!"

Ana buried her face in her mother's white silk riding jacket. The smell of her musky perfume mingled with other smells—sweat, hay, earth.

"This is Lacan," the queen said, indicating the man who was still sitting on his horse. "He is a friend."

"It is a pleasure to meet you, Your Excellency," Lacan said, bowing. He sounded like he was barely older than Ana. "I hear you are leaving for your new school today. You must be very excited."

For some reason, Ana could not find her voice. She buried her face deeper in her mother's jacket.

The queen's fingers dug into her arms. "Tatiana Anatolia, stop acting like a child! Where are your manners?"

"Pleased to meet you," Ana managed to mumble. She looked up at her mother beseechingly. "Momi, I don't want to go!"

"Of course you do. We have discussed this. You must be a brave, strong girl for your mother. Besides, I have arranged for a special surprise for you."

"You have?"

"I have. After you leave here, the carriage will pick up your friend. She and you will ride to the school together."

"You mean Pell?"

"Yes, that's it. Pell."

Ana hugged her mother. "Oh, thank you, Momi! That's such a lovely surprise."

"I'm glad you are happy. It's a mother's job to make her daughter happy." She smiled over her shoulder at Lacan. "Now, Ana, you must go. You must get through the pass by midday in case the rains come."

"Yes, Momi."

Ana hugged her mother one last time, her eyes blurring with tears. *I don't want to go, I don't want to go, I don't want to go,* she wanted to cry out. But she knew her duty, and her mother's wishes for her. And so she grasped Omi's hand and let her help her onto the carriage—Omi whispering, "You be good, child, and listen to your teachers," in a quivering voice—and sank down in the cold leather chair, and made herself feel as numb as possible. She was only dimly aware of the cracking of the whip, the driver's "giddyup, you beasties," and the slow creaking of the carriage wheels, as she turned in her seat and saw Omi standing there, waving like mad, and her mother and the man Lacan already on their horses riding off in the other direction.

Ana was still like this, tears trickling down her face, her heart frozen and quiet, when the carriage pulled up to the Fortunas cottage and Pell jumped up onto the seat beside her and practically tackled her in her exuberance, shouting, "Tati, we're going together! We're going together!" Down below, Pell's mother was on her knees mouthing blessings of gratitude to the queen, and there was the young boy Milo with his big, syrup-sticky grin, and even Stefan in the back, so handsome in his military uniform, calling out his best wishes and Godspeed to the two girls.

Momi, Ana wanted to cry out. *Momi!*

But the carriage was already moving along, and Pell was already talking about their new teachers and their new classes, and by the end of this long, long day, they would reach the school that would be Ana's home for the next ten full moons and beyond.

13

ANDREAS S'ARTE STOOD IN THE FRONT HALLWAY OF THE Academy, not sure of what to do next.

The students would begin arriving shortly. He supposed that the appropriate thing for a headmaster to do would be to conduct one last tour of the building and grounds and check to make sure that everything was in its place—desks and chairs lined up, scribe books in orderly piles, laboratory equipment cleaned and polished. The students' rooms too should be given a final sweep—beds counted, pillows and blankets distributed, windows closed to protect against the coming rains.

But Andreas couldn't seem to move. Inertia had overtaken his body like a pleasant drug.

And so he stood there where he was and studied his surroundings. The front hallway was strange, imposing, impressive; it occurred to him that one could spend days, even longer, studying it. It was a tall, domed room made entirely of white stone. The carvings on the stone were impossibly cryptic: birds foraging for jewels; angels flying through fire; wild animals engaged in mortal combat or a mating dance, it was difficult to tell which.

Directly above him, at the nexus of the ceiling, was the royal crest of Ran. And circling the crest, in gold, was a phrase in old Innish. Old Innish was not one of Andreas's strong suits. But he thought the phrase meant, loosely, "The mind is a sword that must withstand the test of fire."

Andreas smiled.

The sound of footsteps interrupted his idle reverie. He glanced around and saw Madame Delia, one of the teachers, hurrying down the long hall toward him.

"Sir! Sir Andreas! We have a problem in the kitchen!"

Madame Delia wore a long gray dress that swished around her fat, swollen ankles. Her black hair, streaked with white, was held up with dozens of mismatched pins.

Andreas stuffed his hands into his vest pockets and regarded her coldly. He didn't want her—or any of the others—to get the idea that he was easy, approachable, or even gullible because of his young age. "What is it, Madame Delia?"

Madame Delia stopped in front of him, sweating and

breathless. "The hens, sir! The farmer in Galwirth only sent over ten hens. That's not nearly enough to feed all fifty of the girls and the rest of us too!"

"For pity's sake. Can you not send over the boy for the rest of the hens?"

"The boy had to go home to his mother, sir. She's sick with the gout. What are we to do about dinner, then?"

Andreas sighed. "What else is on the menu?"

Madame Delia batted at her sweaty face with a handkerchief. "Yes, sir. That would be millet and turnips."

"Tell the cook to make extra millet and turnips, then. In the future, I wish that you and the others might try to resolve these little emergencies on your own."

"Yes, sir!"

Madame Delia turned on her heels and walked, limping, briskly down the hall. Another teacher, a tall bag of bones named Madame Quin, emerged from one of the classrooms and joined Madame Delia. The two bent their heads together and began whispering, gesturing at each other with their withered hands. They were the only other teachers at the school besides Andreas. It had been decided that a small faculty would be appropriate.

"Crones," Andreas muttered under his breath.

On an impulse, he pushed open the heavy wooden doors and sauntered out into the front garden. The air was thick with the impending rain; it made his skin feel immediately heavy, damp. A cool breeze stirred the leaves on the trees, revealing their pale green undersides. A sign of a coming storm, his mother had taught him when he was a child.

Andreas had not seen his mother in many years. When he was just ten, she had begun accusing him, his father, and the rest of the family of trying to kill her. She slept with a knife under her pillow; once, when Andreas had gone to her in the middle of the night because of a bad dream, she had pointed the knife at his throat. He had managed to escape before she could harm him. His younger brother, Arne, had not been so fortunate.

His mother was in a hospital now, in Catonia or somewhere. His father still lived at the house; he spent his days tending to the garden and talking to the sheep and taking care of Arne, who had no use of his arms. His sister, Esme, disappeared a long time ago. Some said that she had joined a band of Gypsies in a faraway kingdom. Others said she had become addicted to smoking sopa seeds and died.

Just then a black carriage appeared at the edge of the woods. Andreas glanced at his timepiece in annoyance. Early. He hadn't expected any of the students this soon. The carriage entered the gates, pulled by two chestnut horses.

He ran a hand through his hair, feeling suddenly,

inexplicably nervous. But why should he be nervous? He had been courted for this job, and offered what seemed to be a king's ransom in gold for a salary. Arguably, his job description was not a typical one. But he would be able to handle it. And afterward, he would live richly—not in some small village taking care of gardens and sheep, not wasting away with a bunch of sopa-smoking Gypsies, but in one of the big cities, like a nobleman, surrounded by servants, fine food, and lovely women.

The carriage slowed down and stopped.

"Good afternoon to you, sir!" the driver called out. He jumped down from his seat and straightened his wool cap. "Looks like the rain's coming any minute now!"

"Yes, I suppose," Andreas replied. "How many passengers do you bear?"

"Just two, sir. We had a tough ride through the mountains. Wild boars, you know, and the pass was just about flooded over from the melt."

"Yes, yes."

The driver opened the door to help out his passengers. The first one to emerge was a stunningly beautiful creature in red: long blond hair, blue eyes, dimpled cheeks. Andreas raised his eyebrows.

"Hello!" the girl cried out. She smiled, blushed, and offered her hand. "I'm sorry. It's just that I'm so excited to be here! I'm Pell. Pell Fortunas."

"And I am Andreas S'arte, the headmaster of the Academy. My students call me Andreas."

"Okay! Hello, Andreas." Pell pumped his hand.

Then the other passenger emerged. Andreas let go of Pell's hand.

The girl had what must once have been an extraordinary face. Andreas was an expert on such matters and could see this immediately. He could imagine the high, regal bones beneath the puffy cheeks, the delicate ivory skin beneath the sea of blemishes.

Andreas took in the rest of her, swiftly appraising. Her long brown hair was dirty, cut in ragged layers. Her lips were cracked and dry. Her nails were bitten down and bleeding. And her blue-gray dress, as elegant as it was, clearly hid a shapeless, unhappy body.

It had to be her.

Andreas dropped to his knees and bowed his head. "Your Excellency," he murmured. "I bid you a most cordial welcome to the Academy."

He glanced up, waiting for a response. Two large, liquid brown eyes regarded him. She looked like a deer trying to size up danger.

"Please call me Ana," the girl said finally. "And there's no need for the formalities. Here I am your student, and you are my headmaster."

"Of course," Andreas said, rising to his feet. "I bid you a most cordial welcome to the Academy, Ana."

Pell hooked her arm through Ana's and beamed at Andreas. "Andreas, can we look around? Where is the dormitory? Will Ana and I be sharing the same room? Oh, please, *please* say yes!"

Andreas allowed himself to smile. Young girls were so easy to please. "If that is your wish. Let me show you both to the dormitory. Your man can follow with your trunks."

"Yay!" Pell cheered. "Tati, we're going to be living together! Isn't that wonderful? Isn't that the best news ever?"

"Yes, it is," Ana replied, grinning. "Except that your snoring will keep me awake."

"I do not snore!"

"Yes, you do!"

"Liar!"

"Okay, I'm lying!"

The two girls melted in a fit of giggles.

Andreas listened to their back-and-forth as he led them through the door, into the front hallway. *The mind is a sword that must withstand the test of fire.* The birds hunting for jewels, the angels flying through flames, the wild animals killing each other or procreating, seemed to stare down at him.

Beauty

For a moment he thought that they were speaking to him, sending him a message.

And then the moment passed, and the two girls' chatter bubbled up to the surface, and Andreas found himself saying, in a crisp, authoritative voice, "This way, girls." It must have been the wine earlier, or the damp weather, he told himself. He straightened his vest, stuffed his hands into the pockets, and started down the hall toward the dormitory.

14

"IT WAS ON THESE GROUNDS THAT THE GREAT POET PICARDI wrote his finest work. This landscape, and Mother Nature herself, provided him with much of his inspiration."

Andreas paused to consult his notes. Behind him a long, slender branch of cherry blossoms quivered in the breeze.

"He is *so* handsome!" a girl sitting near Ana said to another girl.

"Do you suppose he is married?" the second girl said.

"I don't know! What if he's not?"

"He does live alone in the headmaster's chambers."

"Look at his hair. Have you ever seen a man with such beautiful hair?"

Pell, who was on the other side of Ana, leaned over and whispered, in a high, mocking voice, "Have you ever seen a man with such beautiful hair?"

Ana clamped a hand over her mouth to keep from laughing. Pell grinned at her. Ana squeezed Pell's arm and whispered, "Shhhh! You'll get us both into trouble."

"Andreas doesn't see us. He's too busy striking poses for the girls in the front."

"Shhhh!"

But Ana had to admit that Pell was right. Andreas, with his curly dark hair, chiseled features, and brooding good looks, was an endless object of worship, speculation, and gossip among the students—a fact of which he seemed all too aware. School had been in session for nearly one full moon now. Each afternoon he conducted a special lecture in the sun-filled garden, which allowed him to pontificate in front of fifty—or nearly fifty—adoring girls who sat on the grass in their matching white dresses, listening attentively to his every word on literature, art, and music. Many of them, Ana noticed, did not use their scribe books for taking notes. Instead, they wrote Andreas's name over and over again, or drew doting sketches of his face.

What is *this place, anyway?* Ana wondered, not for the first time. She had expected the Academy to be a walled fortress devoted to education, with a rigorous regime of classes, laboratory work, and field sports far superior to anything she had experienced at the village school.

But so far, their days had consisted mostly of lazy afternoon lectures in the garden, music concerts, and painting lessons in the studio. The other teachers, Madame Delia and Madame Quin, were supposed to lead the History and Science sessions. But these sessions had been postponed, by Andreas's orders, to allow the girls to acclimate to their new environment. "Acclimate," as though they were delicate flowers that had been exposed to a harsh new climate.

Ana had also expected the students to be the most intellectually accomplished in all of Ran. Wasn't that what Pell's letter of invitation had indicated? That the Academy was a special, highly coveted institution for girls with "exceptional academic potential"?

But as far as Ana could tell, most of her fellow students had very little of that. They could not answer Andreas's simplest questions: "What is the poet trying to say with this image? What do these two paintings have in common? Is this musical phrase tonal or atonal? Happy or melancholy?"

The girls were definitely not brilliant.

However, they *were* all beautiful.

Ana had noticed this immediately, on the first day. After she and Pell had settled into the room they were to share, the other girls began to arrive by carriage from their respective villages. At dinner Ana watched one girl after another entering the dining hall; she was startled to see that they were all exceptionally attractive, like Pell. Not one of them could be called fair or average, much less ugly.

Except for her.

At first Ana thought that she was imagining it. Perhaps she had become so insulated, so comfortable in her own hideous shell that she could no longer judge the appearance of other girls clearly and objectively. Perhaps, through her muddled lens, everyone looked beautiful compared to her.

But Pell had noticed it too. "These girls, all they care about is being the prettiest one here," she complained to Ana one day. "And all they talk about is dresses and hairpins and jewelry and face powder. Don't they have anything better to do?"

Ana wondered if she would survive this place.

Andreas paused in the middle of a speech about rhyme schemes and meter and glanced at his timepiece. "All right now, let's take a brief respite! Then we'll gather in the studio to continue working on our canvases."

"Excuse me, Andreas!"

"Wait, Andreas!"

A dozen or more girls jumped to their feet and rushed up to him. They surrounded him like a swarm of white butterflies: flitting, hovering.

"Oh, Andreas! Please, *please* may I carry your books? Shine your boots? Listen to you breathe?" Pell mimicked.

"Come on," Ana said to Pell, laughing. "Let's go get something to eat."

"As long as we can eat alone," Pell replied. "These girls make me crazy!"

"Me too."

Ana and Pell slipped away from the others and went inside to the dining hall. The cook, a short, stout woman with yellow hair and fierce blue eyes, was wiping down the tables.

"What's it you want, girlies?" she called out. "Kitchen's closed."

"Could we possibly have another bowl of your chestnut soup?" Pell pleaded with her. "It's the most delicious thing we've ever tasted! Isn't it, Ana?"

"Oh, yes!"

The cook narrowed her eyes at them. "You're lyin', both of you. Besides, there's none of that soup's left. Well, maybe a spoonful. Let me go see."

The cook disappeared into the kitchen. Pell smiled triumphantly at Ana. "There! I got us some food."

Ana giggled. "What would I do without you, Pella?"

"Starve."

"You're right!"

The two girls sat down across from each other at a

corner table. Ana glanced around the dining hall. It was an enormous white room with tall white columns and crystal chandeliers. The walls were covered with large gilded mirrors.

On the ceiling was an elaborate mural by Ciro, one of the artists Andreas liked to pontificate about. The scene portrayed dozens of naked young women against a backdrop of pink and mauve and pearl-colored clouds. They wore wreaths of flowers on their heads and waved garlands in the air. Ana could never be sure if the young women were dancing or just posing. To her, they looked frozen—trapped.

"So, Tati," Pell said, leaning forward. "What do you think of the Academy, anyway?

Ana shrugged. "It's not what I expected."

Pell nodded. "I know! We hardly have any lessons at all. Andreas is weird. And the other girls are so awful. Especially Gemma and Giselda."

"Who?"

"Gemma and Giselda. You know, the sisters with the long red hair and the pointy noses? I hate them."

Ana grinned. "Why do you hate them?"

"They're rude! And they think they rule this place."

Ana tried to recall the twins. They shared a room down the hall from her and Pell. In their identical white school uniforms, it was hard to tell them apart.

"Gemma is the really evil one," Pell went on. "Do you know what she said about the red dress Grandmomi made for me? In front of everybody? 'Oh, is that what the farm girls are wearing these days?'"

"That *is* rude," Ana agreed.

"And she and Giselda have private parties in their room with some of the others. They trade clothes and beauty herbs and paint one another's faces."

"How do you know all this?" Ana asked her curiously.

Pell shrugged. "Oh, I hear things."

The cook appeared with a tray with two steaming bowls of soup. "Here," she muttered, setting the tray down on the table with a loud *thunk*. "There weren't much soup, just as I says. Here's some bread, too, and goat butter, and elderberry jam. And some radish pickles I makes this morning."

"Thank you!" Pell beamed. "This is so wonderful. Thank you!"

"Yes, thank you," Ana added.

The cook mumbled something under her breath, then disappeared into the kitchen. The soup smelled delicious; Ana lifted a spoonful to her lips. It reminded her of a soup Omi used to make many moons ago, before Ana had started living on little more than stale cloudberry pastries and moldy cheeses.

"This is *so* good," Pell said.

"Mmm."

"Your skin," Pell said suddenly.

Ana frowned. She touched her face. "What's wrong with my skin?"

"Nothing! What I meant was, your skin looks so pretty. Ever since we got here."

Ana turned and stared at herself in a mirror. Pell was right. The ugly red blemishes were fading away. Her cheeks were no longer pasty-looking, but pink and glowing. The fresh air and sunshine and the regular bathing regimen she followed along with the other girls had had an effect on her complexion.

Ana had to resist the impulse to smile. It had been a long time since she hadn't felt the terrible empty feeling when she looked in the mirror.

"Tati?" Pell said worriedly. "Did I say something wrong?"

"No," Ana reassured her. "You didn't say anything wrong at all."

15

⸙

"So . . . you're a princess," Gemma said.

Ana glanced up from her canvas, the painting of the apple she had been working on. It didn't look like an apple, exactly, but more like a small animal: green and dented with black spots like eyes, hovering in a shadowy corner as though preparing to attack.

Gemma and Giselda had set up their easels next to Ana. The other students were spread around the vast, airy art studio. The sisters were as Pell had described them, with long, flowing red hair and sharp, aquiline noses. The quality of their beauty—regal, elegant, cold—reminded Ana of her mother.

Pell was across the studio in an isolated spot, taking advantage of some special angle or some fleeting state of sunlight. Ana wished suddenly that she were not so far away.

Giselda looked up from her painting, which was a perfect imitation of the large, shiny red apple that Andreas had set out on the center table. "Should we call you 'Your Excellency' or something?" she said, smiling pleasantly at Ana.

"No, 'Ana' is fine."

"So, Ana!" Gemma exclaimed, dabbing purplish-red paint onto her canvas. "It must be so amazing to be a princess. You must have dozens of maids and ladies-in-waiting at the palace. Do they take care of you and dress you and brush your hair every morning?"

"That must be so wonderful!" Giselda cried out. "Can you imagine, Gem?"

Ana added another black spot to her apple. Now it had three eyes. "When I was younger. Not anymore. And it wasn't dozens."

"You must have so many lovely, fancy dresses at the palace," Gemma went on. "And sapphires and diamonds and other jewels too. "

"Not really."

Giselda leaned over and regarded Ana with a worried expression. "We sort of noticed that you don't exactly *look* like a princess," she whispered. "To tell you the truth, we figured that you were in disguise. You know, like you didn't want anyone to *know* you were the queen's daughter."

"Yes, we came up with a theory," Gemma said, tossing her hair over her shoulders. "Your mother is forcing you to conceal your true appearance, to keep you safe from danger. After all, she must have enemies everywhere. Maybe even here, at the Academy."

Giselda nodded. "Your mother must love you very much."

"Except—isn't there some other disguise she could have given you?" Gemma said. "It must be so tedious to have to look like that every day."

"Gem!" Giselda cried out.

Ana narrowed her eyes at Gemma. Pell was right; Gemma *was* the more evil of the two sisters.

"It's actually very liberating," Ana replied after a moment. "I would think it would be more tedious to have to look like *you* every day."

Gemma started. "What? What do you mean?"

"Well, what do you look like when you wake up in the morning?" Ana pointed out. "Your hair is tangled and disheveled, right? As though wrens could make a nest in it? How long do you have to spend brushing it so that it is neat and smooth again? And what about your skin, which must smell like stale wool and yesterday's dirt? And your eyes, which must be red and full of sleepy ooze? How long do you have to bathe, how many potions do you have to apply, how many colors do you have to brush onto the raw canvas of your face so you look more like a beautiful painting than the ordinary heap of cells that you really are? That we *all* really are?"

Gemma stared at her, her blue eyes enormous. "That's the craziest thing I've ever heard."

Giselda laughed nervously. "She's teasing you, Gem. Don't you see that she's teasing you?"

"Ladies, let's focus on our canvases!"

Ana turned. Andreas was standing there, his hands clasped behind his back, regarding the three girls' paintings.

"Giselda, that's a lovely apple. Gemma, marvelous use of space," Andreas remarked.

"Thank you, Andreas," the sisters trilled in unison.

Andreas came up to Ana and stood right next to her. Ana could smell a fine, faint fragrance on his skin, like sandalwood. She recalled from Science that sandalwood was the dense yellow heartwood of a parasitic tree.

"Now, Ana," Andreas said with a wide, charming smile. "What do we have here?"

"It's not finished," Ana replied tersely. For some reason, she did not want Andreas to see her painting.

"Your work is rather interpretive, is it not? Instead of being literal?"

"Is that wrong?"

"There is no 'wrong' in art, dear Ana. As long as your

intentions are meaningful, as long as you are challenging yourself."

Ana stared at her painting, frowning. Her intentions were *not* meaningful. She was *not* challenging herself. She was merely painting what she felt: a green apple, black spots, damage, danger.

Andreas touched her elbow and squeezed it, briefly, before moving on to the next girl. Ana did not understand why he felt compelled to touch his students so much. Madame Winks never did that. Perhaps this was part of the intimate, intensive environment of the Academy.

Giselda's voice interrupted her thoughts. "So, would you like to come to a party in our room tonight, Your Ex—I mean, Ana? We're making bracelets and necklaces out of sopa shells—"

"You're wrong, Giselda, we're doing that another night," Gemma interrupted. "Tonight we have to study."

"Gem, what are you talking about?"

"That's okay. I'm not very good at making jewelry, anyway," Ana said quickly.

Giselda began whispering furiously to her sister. Ana resumed painting, in silence. She could occasionally hear Andreas's remarks to the other girls—"Beautiful brushstrokes, Eris!" "Fine use of color, Hali!"—and the giggling, breathless comments in response. At one point

Ana glanced up to see Andreas across the room, standing next to Pell, his arm around her shoulders, her
blond head nodding: *yes, yes, yes.* What was he saying to
her? And why was she acting like that with him?

Perhaps she was just being respectful. Later, when
they were alone in their room, Pell would no doubt
reinterpret the incident for Ana in her usual hilarious,
acerbic way: *And then he said, "You are the finest young artist
I have ever met, Pell, and would you like to see my own canvases later? In the privacy of my chambers?" And I said, "Oh,
Andreas, that is so kind of you to ask but I would rather spend
the evening cutting Gemma and Giselda's toenails. . . ."*

Ana set her brush down and broke into laughter.
Gemma and Giselda stopped whispering and stared at
her as though she were insane.

16

❦

"MAYBE THIS PLACE ISN'T AS BAD AS WE THOUGHT," Pell declared.

Ana squinted, trying to read Pell's expression. With the sun in Ana's eyes, Pell looked as though she were surrounded by a shimmering wall of haze. Bees buzzed around their picnic lunch of black bread, pickles, and goat's cheese. In the distance the flowers in the garden formed a dizzying kaleidoscope of color.

"Pella! What do you mean?" Ana asked her curiously.

"I mean, there are some nice girls here," Pell replied. "Like Nyla and Calla. Did you know that Calla's brother goes to military school with Stefan? And did you know that Nyla is a really talented painter? She's good at card games, too. Not just Kings, but games I've never even heard of."

"Oh."

"Even Andreas isn't so awful," Pell went on. "I mean, he has a very high opinion of himself. And it's so silly how he acts with the girls! But he's not a bad teacher. He's been helping me improve my painting technique. He's been helping me with my poems, too."

"He has?"

"He has!"

"Huh."

Ana pushed her lunch aside and leaned back onto the grass. This was not the speech she had expected from Pell about Andreas. She didn't know what to make of it.

A row of puffy white clouds floated hypnotically across the blue horizon. A peregrine falcon and a glossy black raven circled each other in the air, playing or trying to kill each other—Ana couldn't tell which.

An ant scurried up her arm. Ana didn't bother brushing it off.

Pell leaned back onto the grass too, so that her head touched Ana's. The two of them lay there like that for a long time, still and silent. Ana was confused by Pell's newfound enthusiasm for the school. But maybe Pell had the right attitude. Maybe she, Ana, should be more open-minded about the other students and Andreas. After all, they couldn't *all* be terrible.

"Tati, what are you thinking about?" Pell said after a moment.

"Nothing," Ana fibbed. "What are *you* thinking about?"

"I was just thinking about what it will be like in the future. When you're the queen, that is."

Ana made a face. "Why are you thinking about *that*?"

"Because! This school is supposed to prepare you for being queen. Isn't that what your mother told you?"

Ana sighed. "I'm not even sure I want to be queen."

Pell sat up and regarded Ana with an incredulous expression. "What? Tati, how can you not want to be queen?"

"I just don't. I'd rather be something else. A sculptor, or a poet, or a gamekeeper. Anything."

"Tati, that's sacrilege! You're a princess. You're going to be queen, whether you like it or not."

"Well, I don't like it."

"I don't understand you. Besides, it'll be fine, Tati, because I'll be with you. I could work for you. Maybe as the head of the royal guard."

Ana smiled despite herself. Pell, the head of the royal guard! "You'll have to cut off all your hair," she pointed out.

"Oh, I don't care about my hair."

"And you'll have to start riding again. You haven't

ridden since your accident," Ana reminded her gently.

Pell made a face. "Dracon was a beast! I was lucky it was only my wrist that got broken when he threw me."

"Dracon is crazy," Ana agreed. "She has the blood of her mother, Dendril."

"See? As long as I have a pleasant, well-mannered horse, I wouldn't mind trying to ride again. And if none of the horses suit me, I can be your—let's see—your political adviser or something."

Ana laughed. "Okay, then."

"So we will rule Ran together?"

"We will rule Ran together."

"Handshake."

"Handshake."

The two of them hooked their forefingers together. It had been their childhood handshake for when they traded toys, set off on a treasure hunt, or promised to extract money or favors from their respective parents.

"That's it, then," Pell said, sounding satisfied. "So, Tati. When you become queen, will you keep the strange little man?"

"You mean the odd one who is with my mother all the time?"

"Uh-huh."

Ana frowned. "He scares me. I don't know why, but he scares me. He always has."

"What does he do, anyway?"

"He makes beauty potions for my mother. He dresses her."

"He does? I wish he worked for me, then. Your mother is the most beautiful woman in the world! If only I could look like her!"

Ana gaped at Pell. "But Pella . . . you're so beautiful! Why would you want to look like my mother, or anyone else?"

Pell blushed. "I'm not nearly beautiful enough. My cheeks are too big. My skin is too ruddy. My breasts are the wrong shape."

Ana laughed. "Pella, you're crazy!"

"I am not!"

"You are too."

Pell giggled and nibbled on a piece of black bread. Ana stared at Pell, at her long blond hair and her lovely, angelic face, and wondered what could make her think that she was anything less than perfect. Pell was objectively beautiful, just as Ana was objectively ugly. Or was it not possible to be objective when it came to one's beauty?

The sun emerged from behind a cloud. Ana felt blinded by the sudden brightness and closed her eyes. She tried to imagine the future. She tried to imagine Pell in military uniform, sword in scabbard, her hair shorn like a boy's.

Then she tried to imagine herself dressed in a red and gold gown, presiding at the royal conference table and negotiating treaties, defending borders. Being called "Your Majesty."

And yet . . . her mind would not allow her to go there. She could only become queen if her mother passed away, and that was inconceivable. Queen Veda was so full of life. She was also born to rule, with her incredible wisdom and strength. What did she, Ana, have to offer? She was neither wise nor strong. She did not know how to command respect—command, period. She felt, deep inside, that she was destined for a quiet life in the shadows of the palace, getting her small pleasures where she could: in her cats, her rabbits, Pell.

She would never admit it to Pell. But deep down, she hoped she would never be called upon to become queen, to replace her mother.

17

ANDREAS RECEIVED HIS ORDER IN THE FORM OF A LETTER, accompanied by an elegantly wrapped package. The letter began:

> *It is time for you to introduce your students to Beauty. The package contains everything you need, along with the necessary instructions. . . .*

Andreas read the letter five, six times, in the privacy of his chambers. He had locked the door and given word to the staff not to disturb him under any circumstances. The dormitory was quiet; it was hours past the students' mandatory bedtime.

He had expected the order to come, but not so soon. Only two full moons had passed since the students' arrival at the Academy. He had thought six full moons, at least—but alas, it was not to be. Now his true work would begin. No more long, leisurely afternoons in the garden reading poetry to the wide-eyed young maidens.

Well, perhaps—but those pursuits would have to become secondary.

Which one would he pick first? Andreas mused. Perhaps Nyla, with her golden curls. Or Amara, with her lovely smile. Or Calla, with her silky brown skin. Or perhaps the twins Gemma and Giselda, who thought they knew everything there was to know about beauty. Or any one of the dozens of other girls.

Then he thought of Lilika, with her swanlike figure and black hair. She was always pursuing him after class, asking questions, flirting to get his attention. She would make an excellent first candidate.

Andreas folded the letter carefully and tucked it away in his trunk, under a special silk-lined panel. The flame of his candle trembled and hissed.

He poured himself a goblet of strong wine and downed it. Then another. The liquid burned down his throat and filled his belly with a pleasant warmth.

Still, the wine did not dissipate the sliver of doubt he felt about his assignment. What if he should fail? he wondered. Or worse yet, what if he was never meant to accept this assignment at all?

Andreas sauntered over to the large bay window and stared out at the velvet blackness of the night. There was no moon, no stars—no beacon for him to follow, no sign to tell him what to do.

But Andreas knew what he had to do. He always did. Which was why he was the headmaster of the most prestigious school in the kingdom of Ran, and not a farmer. Or a sopa addict. Or a lunatic.

Andreas returned to his desk and set his empty goblet down.

Then he proceeded to open the package.

18

❧

IT HAD RAINED EVERY DAY FOR THE PAST TWO WEEKS. There had been no outdoor lectures at the Academy lately; instead, the students spent much of their time inside painting still lifes, or listening to harpsichord music, or composing poetry in the manner of Picardi—most of which, Ana had no doubt, were odes to Andreas's hair and eyes.

Ana sat in her room, trying to get through just a few more pages of *The History of the Wars* by the scholar Indra—one of her father's favorites. Her pink blanket, which Omi had packed for her, was draped across her lap. She kept looking out the window, at the rain cascading down the glass and blurring the landscape into wet brushstrokes of color. In the distance a field of dark purple irises bobbed and waved in the wind. Every few minutes lightning flashed and turned the sky into metal.

War is what human beings do to each other when there is no morality left, Indra wrote.

Ana heard a noise at the door. "Pell?" she called out eagerly.

Footsteps receded down the hallway. A door opened and closed.

Ana frowned and returned to her book. Where was Pell? She had not seen her all afternoon, not since sculpture class.

Actually, she had not seen much of Pell in the last few days. She went out a great deal, and returned to their room only to sleep. She seemed to spend a lot of time with the other girls, especially Calla and Nyla.

But what is morality? Who is to determine what is right and what is wrong? Some may argue that taking the life of an individual may be justified if it is for the greater good.

Ana ran her finger down the worn, dog-eared page. The book had belonged to her father, and before that, his father, and so on. What had gone through Galen's mind, reading and re-reading Indra's words? Ana knew he had led many battles and killed many enemy soldiers—maybe even civilians, during the uprisings in the mountain villages.

Was this a choice she would have to face someday? To take the life of an individual—the lives of many individuals—for the greater good?

But she didn't want to think about such a serious

subject. She wanted to find Pell and talk about silly things: Andreas's pet pupils, Picardi's poems, Madame Delia's hairpin collection. She got up abruptly, set her book down, and walked out the door.

She headed down the long hallway, wondering where Pell could be. Perhaps in the dining hall? Perhaps in the art studio? Everything was quiet except for the steady drumbeat of raindrops on the roof. Occasionally Ana could hear heated voices or a loud peal of laughter in the distance.

Ana turned the corner. She saw that the door to one of the dormitory rooms was partially open—Gemma and Giselda's. There was giggling and chatter coming from within.

Ana peered inside. She saw Pell sitting on a bed, between Calla and Nyla. Gemma and Giselda were sitting on the other bed.

Ana frowned. Gemma and Giselda? What was Pell doing with *them*?

She hesitated, then knocked. "Hello?"

"Come in!" someone called out.

Ana entered. The room was cheerfully disheveled. Every surface, every inch of the floor was covered with piles of velvet and silk, long beaded necklaces, pots of beauty cream. The air was thick with the fragrance of flowers and herbs.

"Tati!" Pell cried out. She rushed up to Ana and

hugged her. "You're missing out on all the fun!"

Ana pulled back and smiled curiously at Pell. "Fun? What fun?"

"We've been playing dress-up!" Calla piped up. "See?"

She, Nyla, Gemma, and Giselda all rose to their feet and gathered around Pell. Posing side by side like that, the five girls looked amazingly similar. They were dressed in matching white lace dresses. They wore long strings of crystal beads—purple, magenta, violet, lavender—wrapped around and around their necks. They wore identical silver powder on their eyelids and rose-pink paint on their lips.

"What do you think, Tati?" Pell asked her.

"You all look so beautiful," Ana said, meaning it.

It wasn't just their costumes and makeup. All the girls seemed to have an uncharacteristic glow about them. Their eyes sparkled. Their complexions were radiant. Their hair seemed especially full and lustrous.

Ana gazed at them in wonder. They were perfectly, identically beautiful—even more beautiful than usual. And for a moment, she felt the familiar pang of longing: to be like them, to be breathtakingly lovely, to move with the languid, easy grace of total self-assurance. What would it be like? She would probably never know.

Gemma came up to Ana and hugged her. "We're so

glad you're here! Do you want to join us?"

Ana stared at Gemma, confused. Why was she being so nice to her?

"Yes, yes! Please stay," Nyla begged.

"We won't take no for an answer," Calla added.

Ana shook her head. She had no place here with these five beautiful girls, playing dress-up. "I can't. I have to study—," she began.

Pell draped a string of sopa beads around Ana's neck. "We won't let you, Tati. You *have* to stay. We are going to make you beautiful!"

"Yes!"

"Let's put flowers in her hair!"

"Who has the silver powder?"

"I get to paint her!"

"No, let me!"

Ana felt two, four, six hands gently pushing her down into a chair. Then someone draped more beads around her neck, and someone else began brushing her hair, and yet another person laid a warm, scented cloth across her face, erasing her vision. Ana took a deep breath, trying to still the intense anxiety she suddenly felt.

And yet she felt something else, too. Pleasure. It was a long time since anyone had brushed her hair, or painted her face, or taken an interest in her appearance at all.

"Just relax," someone commanded. Ana wasn't sure who.

She took another deep breath and tried to obey.

"Tati," Pell whispered. "Are you awake?"

Ana blinked into the darkness. It was nearly pitch black, with just a thin slant of moonlight illuminating the room. She had no idea what time it was.

"I'm awake. Are you awake?" Ana whispered back.

"Yes."

"Can't you sleep?"

"No! I'm too excited."

"About what?"

Ana heard the rustling of blankets, then the quiet *thud* of Pell's feet landing on the floor. A moment later Pell lay down next to her and slipped under the covers, giggling.

"Wasn't that fun today, Tati? With Calla and the other girls?"

"I suppose."

"Wasn't it fun to be . . . to be beautiful again?"

Ana frowned. "I was *not* beautiful, Pella. Far from it. It would take more than fancy clothes and face paint."

"But you *could* be beautiful again," Pell persisted.

Ana sat up slightly and stared at Pell. "What are you talking about? Why are you so interested all of a sudden in playing dress-up and makeup, anyway?

"It's more than that," Pell replied enigmatically. "Can I tell you a secret?"

"A secret?"

"Yes!"

Pell's voice had an undeniable edge to it. It was excitement, and energy, and something else, too. Agitation.

"Pella? What is it?" Ana asked her.

"There's a new beauty potion," Pell explained. "Some of the girls have tried it. Calla, Nyla, Gemma, Giselda, and others. Lilika, Hali. It's incredible, Tati! It doesn't just make you *look* more beautiful. It makes you *feel* beautiful too. Inside. Like everything is wonderful."

"Where did you get this beauty potion?" Ana asked her curiously. "Did you and the other girls make it?"

Pell shook her head. "No, no. It comes in a little pill that you have to take. Every day. Here, I want you to try it." She reached into the pockets of her nightgown and began digging around.

"It's a beauty potion in a little pill?" Ana said. "I've never heard of anything like that."

"Here it is, Tati! Just put it on your tongue and swallow it."

Ana felt Pell place the tablet on her lips. What could it hurt to try it? she thought. Pell seemed to believe in its powers. And from what Ana had seen of Calla, Nyla, and the twins earlier today, the medicine seemed to work. They had all been glowing, radiant.

Ana parted her lips. On her tongue, the pill tasted sweet and dry and powdery, like a kind of candy her mother used to give her when she was little.

Just swallow, she told herself.

But some impulse, some reflex, made her flinch and spit it out.

"Tati, what are you doing?" Pell cried out. "You've wasted it!"

"It tasted funny," Ana lied. "Maybe I'll try another one tomorrow."

"That was my last one!"

"I'm sorry, Pell. Can't you get more?"

"I don't know. Oh, Tati!"

Pell wriggled out of the covers, got up, and returned to her own bed. "Good night, Tati," she mumbled. Her voice sounded angry, irritated.

"Pella, I'm sorry!"

Pell didn't reply. Ana wanted to keep talking to her, to ask her more questions about this new beauty potion. But she couldn't bring herself to say anything more. Pell seemed so annoyed, which was not like her.

And yet—why had Ana spit the medicine out? Why had she refused Pell's offer? After all, Pell *was* her closest—her only—friend. She cared about Ana and wanted the best for her.

Perhaps she, Ana, had grown too comfortable with her own ugliness. Perhaps it was time to consider new options, especially now that she was ensconced in this school, so far away from her mother.

Ana lay there for a long time in the darkness, unable to sleep, listening to the sound of Pell breathing and murmuring nonsense words in her dreams.

19

A GREAT GENERAL POSSESSES SEVERAL IMPORTANT CHARACteristics. One: The ability to feel fear. Two: The ability to ignore it.

It was the sixth time Ana had read this passage. She still did not understand it. What was Indra talking about? How could one feel fear and ignore it at the same time?

She sighed and stared out the window. After many weeks, the long, rainy spell had come to an end. In its wake the garden seemed almost too green, too lush; there were so many leaves, so many flowers, everything thick and dense and jungle-like. Ana reminded herself that she should go for a walk later on, after so many days of being stuck inside.

Ana heard voices in the hallway. Just then the door burst open. Pell walked in, followed by two girls Ana barely knew, Lilika and Hali.

"Tati!" Pell shouted happily. She rushed up to Ana and threw her arms around her neck.

Ana flinched. Pell was squeezing her too tightly. Drawing back, she managed a weak smile and said, "Hi, Pella. Hi, Lilika, Hali."

"Your Excellency!" Hali said, waving.

And then Ana noticed the girls' appearance. Pell and her friends were dressed in matching black silk dresses that were several sizes too big for them. There were dozens of sopa bead wrapped around their necks. Their eyelids were painted thickly with black.

"Well, Tati? What do you think?" Pell cried out.

"That's really . . . pretty," Ana said. Which was the furthest thing from the truth. The girls looked strange, bizarre. Lilika especially looked pale and gaunt, as though she had lost weight. Her black attire only accentuated her wan appearance.

"We're not pretty. We're works of art!" Pell said, twirling around.

"Masterpieces," Lilika agreed.

"Let's show Andreas!" Hali said suddenly. She swiped at her nose with the back of her sleeve. "We can show him our new necklaces, too."

Lilika nodded. "Yes, let's!"

Pell grabbed Ana's hand. "Tati, do you want to come with us? We could paint your eyelids black too. It's really fun!"

Hali raised her hand in the air, as though she were in class. There was a large pool of sweat underneath her armpit. "Let *me* paint her. I want to paint the princess!" she cried out.

"Well, Tati?" Pell said hopefully.

Ana met Pell's eyes. They seemed too eager, too anxious, too *something*. Ana didn't know what that meant. In any case, she didn't want to participate in their game.

"I-I have to finish my book," she said, finally. "You go without me. I'll see you later."

Pell stuck out her lower lip. "Oh, Tati. Okay, if you must."

"See you later?"

"Yes, later!"

Ana gave Pell a small wave and turned her attention back to her book. "I thought her name was Ana or something," she heard Lilika whisper to Pell.

"It is. Tati is her nickname."

"Oh!"

"You two are best friends, aren't you?"

"Have you ever been inside the palace?"

"What is the queen like?"

"Is she as beautiful as they say?"

"Why does *she* dress like that?"

The voices faded and disappeared down the hall.

They're just stupid, Ana told herself. *They're just stupid, stupid girls.*

But somehow this knowledge didn't lift her spirits. What had happened to Pell? Why was she acting like this—like one of *them*? Ana bit her lip and turned to the next page in her book.

The light was starting to fade outside. It would be evening soon—dinnertime. Ana and Pell always sat together in the great dining hall. But perhaps things would be different from now on. Pell might want to sit with Hali and Lilika and Calla and Nyla and all her other new friends instead. Of course she would insist that Ana join them, would not take no for an answer, would make a loud, boisterous scene out of it.

In times of war, one learns the most from one's enemies, not from one's allies.

Ana closed the book and put it down. She got up and walked over to her trunk.

The rusty metal hinges creaked as she opened it. The smells of lavender and cedar wafted up from the neatly folded garments.

Ana began rummaging through the contents. She found the blue-gray dress with the cream-colored lace trim. She also pulled out a blue silk ribbon, stiff with newness, and a silver box full of cosmetics.

Ana laid all these things out on her bed.

Then she sat down and stared at them for a long time. Thinking.

20

❧

QUEEN VEDA SANK BACK INTO HER SILK PILLOWS, SIGHING with pleasure as Brun and Balto massaged her feet. The twins were in rare form today, hitting just the right spots, applying just the right amount of pressure, not annoying her in the least.

The Beauty Consultant was sitting at the dressing table, mixing herbs and crushed spider eggs in a glass jar. He was humming some sort of chant under his breath, or singing to himself—the queen didn't particularly care, as long as the end result was one of his extraordinary formulas.

The Beauty Consultant had been particularly inspired lately, experimenting with new combinations: hare's blood and heather, convolvulus and snakeskin, rosemary and fly's wings. And little by little, day by day, she could feel her former beauty—her former perfection—returning. Everything about her glowed: her skin, her hair, her eyes. Even her body felt slimmer, tighter, like a young girl's body. She noticed the Beauty Consultant staring at her often, his hooded eyes burning red with approval. And the men, Lacan and the others, needed little encouragement to visit her these days.

It felt like a new era in her life, a fresh start.

It had been a glorious idea sending Ana away.

Then the queen remembered the letter. She had received it yesterday, by courier, but had not had a chance to read it yet. She reached across the bed and picked up the unopened envelope from her night table.

The boys looked up at her quickly to make sure that she was not displeased. "The calves," she told them, smiling, as she slit open the envelope with her fingernail.

She pulled out the letter and began reading the tiny, familiar scrawl:

Dearest Momi,

I miss you so much! I know I shouldn't say that. But it seems strange, being away from you for so long. I know it has only been three full moons. But it feels like many more than that.

The Academy is a beautiful place, and you were so kind to send me here. Pell is doing well. She has made many new friends here. I am trying to make new friends too. But Pell is much nicer and friendlier than I am so it is hard for me sometimes.

Still, I am happy and grateful to be here. Thank you, Momi, for arranging that. You always know what is best for me.

I wrote you before about the headmaster, Andreas. All the girls here are in love with him because he is handsome and reads poetry about Solitude and Longing and all that. I am not in love with him at all, though, so please don't worry! I spend most of my time in class or reading books or walking around the garden. The garden has your favorite flower, the red one with the big petals and black spots. What are they called? I will bring some home to you, when I come visit.

How are you? I hope you are well. How is Omi? Please tell her thank you for remembering to pack the pink blanket. It can be cold here sometimes, in the evenings.

I will write again soon.

I miss you!

With love,

your daughter

By the time the queen was done reading the letter, the pale pink paper had become blotched with the oil from her hands. Some of the words were smudged and blurry.

The queen read the letter one more time, just to make sure. Good. Nothing had changed. She ripped the letter in half and let the pieces flutter to the floor.

"Your Majesty?" Brun said, concerned.

"Don't worry, it's excellent news," the queen replied. "You may work on my shoulders now."

"Of course, Your Majesty."

The queen let Brun and Balto slip their hands under her naked body and turn her over, slowly. She listened to the Beauty Consultant's strange little song, the rhythmic sound of his metal spoon clinking against the glass jar as he stirred his herbs and his dead spiders. It felt, at that moment, as though all the beneficent forces in the universe were directed at her. They were conspiring to make her—to *keep* her—the fairest woman in the kingdom. Which was as it should be.

Queen Veda closed her eyes and took a deep breath. For the first time in a long time, she thought about Galen. And smiled.

21

⚜

THE BATH WAS HEAVENLY.

Morning sunlight slanted through the windows and made dappled patterns on the white tiles. Rose petals floated in the water. Scented steam filled the air.

She picked up a bar of honey soap and ran it over her arms, her belly, her legs. She made a handful of lather and ran the bubbles through her hair. With a small brush, she scrubbed vigorously at her feet and her elbows.

She leaned her head back in the water and let her hair billow out around her, like a fan. Ocean sounds gurgled in her ears. In the light, her skin looked pearly, almost translucent.

When she closed her eyes, her eyelids became the color of fire: red, orange, black, gold. Thoughts, dreams, memories drifted around in her head like the rose petals in the bath water. She heard, or imagined she heard, birdcalls, butterfly wings. Words and phrases swirled around, giving birth to poems. The poems were silly and spontaneous and happy; they made her laugh.

And then a poem came to her—not a silly one, but an ancient text she had studied long ago in school:

> *There is beauty in the unlikeliest places.*
> *In the mossy underside of a forgotten gray rock,*
> *In a dry brown field that used to nourish flowers,*
> *and could yet again,*
> *In the cry of a dying bird as its spirit, instead,*
> *ascends to the sky.*
>
> *There is beauty in the unlikeliest places.*
> *I feel it now. There is breath and life inside these*
> *ashes,*
> *A chord trembling into song where there had long*
> *been silence,*
> *A sibyl emerging from her crystal ball and flying,*
> *almost fearless, into the future.*

A sibyl. What was a sibyl? Some sort of a prophet or fortune-teller, she recalled. That's what she would be. A prophet, foreseeing—what? Right now she was immersed in the present, in sunlight, in rose-scented warmth. She could not imagine what her future might hold for her. Nor did she care.

When she finally made herself get out, she dried off her hair and body with a cloth. A single rose petal clung damply to her hand. Giggling, she decided to let it stay. She draped herself with a pink robe and returned to her room.

There, she finished the rest of her ablutions. With a pair of small sewing scissors, she cut her hair—slowly, one strand at a time—until it was a uniform length again. She trimmed her fingernails and toenails so they were smooth, moon-shaped curves. She applied pale pink paint to her cheeks and lips, and pale blue paint to her eyelids. The pots had never been opened, until now.

Finally she pulled the blue-gray dress over her head. She eased the lace-trimmed sleeves over her wrists. Then she tied back her glistening hair with the blue silk ribbon. The rose petal fell off her hand and fluttered to the floor.

When she was done, she glanced at herself in the full-length mirror.

She looked . . . beautiful.

At first the realization struck her like the opposite of warmth—like a plunge into icy water, like a bad dream. Her heart felt as though it would burst out of her chest. Why had she done this? It was too risky, knowing what she knew about her mother. She was breaking the unspoken agreement.

But as much as she wanted her mother's love, she also wanted to be with Pell. She wanted to fit in with Pell's new friends, to fit in at this new place.

She glanced in the mirror again. Her heart steadied, her panic subsided, some of the iciness melted away.

She *was* beautiful.

She had almost forgotten. She had almost forgotten too what it was like to admire oneself in the mirror. It was a giddy thing. Irresistible, really. She admired the way her skin glowed, her hair glowed, her eyes glowed. It was as though she had come to life after a seemingly endless hibernation and shed her dark, dirty winter coat.

Her lips twitched. She smiled.

She could not wait to show Pell.

Queen Veda woke up screaming.

"What is it, Your Majesty?" One of the maids came running through the door, her apron strings flying behind her. "Are you ill? Should I get the doctor?"

"It's nothing," the queen replied, in a voice barely above a whisper. "I had a bad dream, that's all."

22

❧

For Ana it was strange—and wonderful—walking around the halls of the Academy with her new appearance. She had to remind herself to stand straight, shoulders back—not hunched over in a sad, protective curve, which had been her posture for so long now. Every once in a while she caught sight of her reflection in a mirror, or a window, and experienced a small thrill of surprise. *Is that me? Truly?* It was almost embarrassing how light-hearted this superficial change made her feel.

As she searched for Pell she passed other girls in the hallways. Some of them stared at her; some of them didn't even seem to notice her. Ana had expected a few raised eyebrows or teasing comments. *Hey, princess, what happened? Did someone cast a spell on you? When do you turn back into a toad?* But no one said a word.

As she passed one of the classrooms, she noticed several girls inside: Gemma, Giselda, Calla, and Nyla. They were sitting on the floor, playing a card game.

Ana walked into the room. "Excuse me. Has anyone seen Pell?"

Nyla glanced up. Her face looked pale and sweaty. "I'm sorry, but we're not receiving visitors," she said in a slow, stilted voice. "We're not feeling well."

"What's wrong?" Ana asked, concerned.

"Do you have any?" Calla asked Ana eagerly.

Ana frowned. "Any what?"

"Say, 'Do you have any, *Your Excellency*'!" Gemma corrected Calla, giggling.

Giselda wiped her nose with her sleeve. "Forget about it. She doesn't."

"I don't . . . *what*?" Ana said, confused.

"You don't have any, *Your Excellency*," Gemma said. The four girls began laughing hysterically.

"Oh no, I have to throw up," Nyla said suddenly. She leaned over and opened her mouth, letting out a thin stream of yellow bile.

"That's disgusting," Giselda groaned.

Calla clamped her hand over her mouth. "I have to throw up too," she gasped. She began gagging and heaving, her eyes filling with tears.

The rank smell of vomit filled the air. Ana covered

her nose and turned to leave. "I'm going to go get Andreas."

"Andreas is busy," Giselda replied. "He is so, so busy."

"Just wait here."

Ana left the room, her head spinning. Was there a fever going around the school? She wondered if she, too, would catch it. She touched her stomach, then her forehead, then the back of her neck. Her skin did feel a little clammy.

Where could Andreas be? On an impulse Ana went to the front entrance and headed outside. Perhaps Andreas was in the garden, giving an impromptu lecture to some of the girls.

Ana rushed past the purple irises, the stone bridge, the grove of cherry trees. The cherry blossom petals danced in the breeze and fluttered to the ground, their whiteness tinged with the barest blush of pink.

Just then Ana spotted Andreas.

He was on the other side of the garden, past the cherry trees, walking slowly and leisurely toward the forest. There was a girl next to him. Andreas was waving his hands in the air as he did when he was lecturing.

Ana hurried her steps. She saw Andreas put his arm around the girl's slender waist and say something to her. The girl's shoulders shook with laughter.

"Andreas!" Ana shouted, breaking into a run. "Andreas!"

Andreas and the girl paused and turned around.

The girl was Pell.

Ana's heart felt as if was going to explode in her chest. She stopped, almost stumbling on the hem of her dress as she did so. What was Pell doing with Andreas? Why were the two of them acting so—*intimate*?

Andreas whispered something in Pell's ear. Pell's head bobbed up and down. He took Pell's elbow and led her to Ana.

"Hello, Ana," Andreas said. He glanced at her face and her hair. His eyes widened in surprise, but he made no comment. "Out on a stroll, are you? I was just showing Pell the new baby bluebirds. Have you seen them?"

"No," Ana replied. "Pell? Are you all right?"

Pell didn't answer. Ana could tell there was something wrong with her. Her long blond hair was disheveled. Her eyes were red, as though she had been crying.

Ana reached for Pell's hand. "Pell, are you sick too?"

"I'm not sick," Pell replied, wrenching her hand away. "I'm fine! Aren't I fine, Andreas?"

"I must tend to some business," Andreas said abruptly. "I'll see both of you later, in class."

"Calla and Nyla are sick," Ana said quickly to Andreas. "That's why I was looking for you. They threw up."

Andreas raised his eyebrows. "Oh? Well, then, I must see to them immediately."

"Don't forget your medicine, Dr. Andreas!" Pell giggled.

"Pell Fortunas, get hold of yourself," Andreas snapped. He turned and left.

"Pell, what's going on?" Ana demanded when Andreas was out of earshot. "What were you doing out here with Andreas?"

"Looking at the birds," Pell replied.

Pell's bloodshot eyes followed Andreas as he disappeared through the front door. Then they scanned the woods, as if searching for some distant point through the trees.

"'The hunter knows no rest, for the hawk has plundered the nest,'" Pell quoted. "That's early Picardi!"

"Early, *bad* Picardi," Ana agreed. "Pell, let me get you to our room. I think you have the same thing the other girls have."

"Calla has this too?" Pell asked her curiously. "And Nyla?"

Ana nodded.

"Oh, Tati." Pell said, swooning suddenly. "I'm dizzy. I need to sleep, I think."

Ana grabbed Pell and steadied her. "I've got you, Pella. I'll get you into bed. Don't worry."

"Thank you, dear Tati."

Ana put her arm around Pell's shoulders. Pell leaned

against Ana and buried her head in her shoulder. Ana almost recoiled. Pell's skin smelled bad, sour, as though she had not washed in days.

"Okay, take a step. I'll help you," Ana told her.

"You smell good," Pell muttered. "You smell like flowers."

"Try to take a step, Pella."

"'Kay."

Pell hobbled forward. Ana hobbled with her. Together, the two walked toward the front door with excruciating slowness. As Pell babbled incoherently about baby birds and hunters and Picardi, Ana thought of Omi and wished that she were there. Omi would know what to do. She would collect Pell and the other sick girls and tuck them into their beds. She would wash their hot, pale faces with cold cloths and concoct healing potions out of herbs. Omi had always done this for Ana, feeding her remedies made of angelica and bloodroot and wild ginger, comforting her through her fever dreams.

Ana had never nursed anyone back to health, except one of the rabbits once when she had eaten an entire tree branch, and Jax when he had refused water for three days. Animals, yes—but she had never taken care of a person. She had no idea even how to begin. She tried to remember Omi's recipe: two parts angelica, one part bloodroot, and how much wild ginger, boiled for how long? She wished she had paid closer attention. But Omi had always been there, had always done these things automatically from memory, with no help from anyone.

"I need Beauty," Pell said suddenly, interrupting Ana's thoughts.

Ana started. "What?"

"I haven't had any in days. I think that's what's making me sick."

"What do you mean, you need beauty?" Ana asked her curiously. "You *are* beautiful."

"No, I mean Beauty the pill," Pell corrected her. "The wonderful, wonderful pill. Do you have any?"

Do you have any?

Any what?

Say, "Do you have any, Your Excellency"!

Forget about it. She doesn't.

I don't . . . what?

Ana stared at Pell in alarm. "Beauty" must be the name of the pill that Pell had offered her the other night. And it must be what Calla had asked her for.

What was Beauty, exactly?

And what was it doing to Pell—and Calla, and all the other girls?

23

❦

"**W**HAT ARE YOU READING, ANA?"

Ana glanced up from her book. Andreas was standing there, his hands in his pockets, smiling down at her. She was sitting in the hallway on an old bench made of velvet and carved wood.

Ana frowned and closed her book swiftly. She was not in the mood to converse with anyone, especially Andreas.

She also did not want to let him know that she was reading an herbology textbook. For the last two days, she had been searching for references to Beauty. So far, she had been unsuccessful.

"The History of the Wars," she lied, not meeting his eyes.

"Ah, Indra. Yes, he is an interesting one. 'War is what immoral people do to each other,'" Andreas quoted.

"Actually—," Ana began.

"Yes?"

"That's close. But not exactly. Indra wrote, 'War is what human beings do to each other when there is no morality left.'"

Andreas beamed. "That changes the entire meaning, doesn't it? You are a true intellectual, Ana. In fact, that is what I have come to talk to you about."

"It is?"

"Take a walk in the garden with me, Ana. I wish to discuss your academic performance with you."

"You do?"

Andreas offered his hand. Ana hesitated, then allowed him to help her to her feet. *Where are your manners, Tatiana Anatolia?* she could hear her mother saying. Her mother, who had yet to respond to one of her letters.

Andreas began walking down the hall. Ana tucked her herbology book under her arm and fell into step beside him. After a few moments they emerged through the front door into the garden. The air was cool and fragrant with the scent of wild roses.

Andreas plucked one of the roses and lifted it to his face, inhaling. "So how is your friend, Pell? Is she feeling better?"

"I don't know. I think she has the same thing the other girls have. She's been sleeping a lot."

Ana didn't want to bring up what Pell had said about

the pills. She didn't want to get Pell or the others in trouble for taking a beauty potion that may have made them sick.

"Fatigue, yes. The doctor mentioned that that was one of the symptoms of the illness," Andreas said.

"Doctor? What doctor?"

"Her Majesty was kind enough to send the royal doctor from the palace. He observed all the girls who were symptomatic. He said they would all be well soon, with rest."

Ana started. "My . . . mother knows about this? How did she find out? When was Dr. Bezir here? Why didn't he come see me?"

Andreas held up his hands. "I sent Her Majesty a message by special courier, informing her of what seemed to be a virus spreading around the school," he explained. "She had asked to be kept informed of such matters. She responded immediately by sending Dr. Bezir. He came late at night, did his tour, and was gone by sunrise. I believe he had a birth to attend to, back at the palace."

"Oh."

Ana took a deep breath. She felt a sense of relief. Her mother had intervened in her usual powerful, all-knowing way.

And more importantly, the pill called Beauty had not

caused the sicknesses. Obviously it was just another harmless beauty potion.

Andreas put his hand on Ana's arm. "In any case, please don't worry about your friend or the others. They will be fine, in time. Now, I wish to talk about *you*."

Andreas's hand felt soft and warm where he touched her. Ana thought she should move away. Seeing the way Andreas acted around Pell had made her intensely uncomfortable.

But he was her headmaster, and she was his pupil. Perhaps it would be considered bad manners to move away. Ana stayed where she was, and continued to walk by his side.

"Your performance here at the Academy has been exemplary," Andreas went on. "I think it's safe to say that you are one of our finest pupils here. If not *the* finest."

Ana was not sure what Andreas meant. It had taken little effort to meet his amorphous academic standards. The classes here had been meager at best. Ana learned more from reading her own books, and taking long walks on her own, observing plants and insects and animals, than she did sitting through one of Andreas's lectures. And as for Madame Quin and Madame Delia, Ana had yet to see them conduct a Science or History session. In fact, she rarely saw them around. They seemed to sequester themselves in their rooms, planning lessons that never materialized. This week Andreas had sent them away, along with the cook, to visit relatives in various distant villages.

"Thank you," Ana said, finally. She wasn't sure what else she *could* say.

"Come this way," Andreas said, squeezing her arm. "There is a lovely sculpture I wish to show you inside the maze. Made by Ciro himself."

"The painter?"

Andreas nodded. "He was also a sculptor. Only two of his pieces remain, though. The rest were destroyed in the last war, by the Patim warlords."

"Oh."

Ana had never been in the maze, which consisted of high hedges with bluish-green leaves that wound around in a complicated serpentine pattern. Pell had told her once that it was called "Lovers' Maze" because a former mistress of the house, when the Academy had been a private residence, used to rendezvous there with her lover—hidden from view and impossible to find, especially by her drunken husband.

Now Andreas was taking Ana through the maze. Squaring her shoulders, she made a mental note to memorize the path: right, left, left, right, a broken branch here, an untrimmed hedge there.

After a few minutes they emerged into a clearing. In the center of the clearing were a stone bench and a marble statue of a woman. The woman's left arm was missing, and her mouth had been crushed flat.

"Ah, here we are!" Andreas announced cheerfully. "Come, Ana, let us sit."

Ana obeyed. She noticed that the air had grown cooler, and that the sun was growing faint against the purplish-gray sky. It would be evening soon. Shivering, she wrapped her blue wool shawl more tightly around her shoulders.

"Ana," Andreas said. He sat down on the bench next to her. "I mentioned your academic performance earlier. But I have noticed something else about you since you have been here. "

"You have?"

"Forgive me for being blunt. When you first came to the Academy, I had the feeling that you were trying to hide your beauty from the world." Andreas paused and smiled. "But lately, I have noticed that you are no longer trying to hide it. You have let it emerge again."

Ana felt her cheeks burning. How could Andreas—a grown man, a teacher—talk to her like this?

"I'm sorry if this embarrasses you," Andreas said, lowering his voice. "I merely wanted to acknowledge this gift you are giving to yourself. The gift of beauty. You must enjoy it, and you must not feel ashamed."

Ana could barely find her voice. "Oh," she croaked. "Thank you. Now, if that's all, I really must—"

❖

"One more thing," Andreas interrupted. "I can help you."

"Help me?" Ana said, confused.

"I can help you achieve the physical perfection you seek," Andreas went on.

Ana stared at Andreas, dumbfounded, as he reached into the pocket of his vest and pulled out a silver box. He opened the box. Inside was a small pink pill.

"Wh-what's that?" Ana asked him. But she already knew.

"This is a very special drug, called Beauty," Andreas replied. "It is the beauty formula that the world has been searching for since the beginning of time. It will make you more beautiful than you can ever imagine."

Ana's breath caught in her throat. She understood now, all too well.

Pell and the others were getting their supply of Beauty from Andreas. He had told them that it would make them even more beautiful than they already were. But instead, it had made them very, very sick. Andreas had lied to her about Dr. Bezir being here, to cover up.

Andreas lifted the pill to her mouth. "Here you go, my lovely Ana," he whispered. "Just swallow it. It's not bitter at all."

Ana tasted the familiar powdery sweetness of the pill on her lips, just barely, before she spit it out. "No!" she blurted out. "I don't want your medicine!"

Andreas stared at her, his eyes wide and disbelieving. "You dare to refuse Beauty?" he demanded.

Ana pushed Andreas away and jumped to her feet.

"Ana!" Andreas shouted. "Where are you going?"

Clutching her book to her chest, Ana ran as fast as she could into the winding, brambly darkness of the maze.

As Ana ran, staggering, inside the Academy, she caught sight of Lilika. Lilika was leaning against a marble column, staring blankly at a painting of two young boys. She looked pale and sickly. She seemed even thinner and gaunter than she had the last time Ana saw her.

"Lilika!" Ana called out. "Are you all right?"

"What?" Lilika pushed a strand of greasy black hair out of her face. Her eyes looked glazed, confused.

Ana groaned. The Beauty illness was spreading.

"Let me help you to your room," Ana offered.

Lilika covered her face with her hands. She looked as though she were about to burst into tears.

Ana touched her arm. "Lilika! What's wrong?"

In response, Lilika swatted at Ana like an angry cat. "Leave me alone! Just go away, all right?"

"But—"

Lilika had left a deep red scratch on Ana's hand. Ana wiped the blood against her skirt and glanced around. There was no one else nearby. She didn't know what to do.

"I'll be back, okay?" Ana told Lilika. "Stay here."

Lilika didn't reply. She slid down the marble column slowly, making tiny weeping sounds, and slumped down on the floor.

Ana bent down and grasped Lilika's shoulders. "Did you take the pills? Did you take Beauty?" she asked her.

Lilika stared at her, her eyes suddenly alert. "Did Andreas give you some?" she said eagerly.

Ana's heart sank. "No—," she began.

"Give me some!" Lilika said, her voice suddenly harsh. "Give me some right now, or I'll kill you! *Do you hear me?*"

Ana rose to her feet and took a few steps back. "I'm going to get some help, okay?" she said, trying to sound calm. "Stay here. I'm going to get some help."

Ana turned and began hurrying down the hallway. She felt despair washing over her, and she had to bite her lip to keep from crying. Who was going to help her? Not Pell or any of the other girls. Not the cook or Madame Delia or Madame Quin, who were away on holiday. And certainly not Andreas.

Just then Ana made a decision. She would ride out at first light to return to the palace. It was time for her mother, for the queen, to know what was going on at the Academy. And to intervene, as only the queen of Ran could.

24

✦

QUEEN VEDA SAT AT THE WINDOW, SIPPING A CUP OF TEA. It was one of the Beauty Consultant's latest concoctions, consisting of lemon balm, garlic, vinegar, and a large amount of honey to mask the taste. Unfortunately the honey was not doing its work. Grimacing, the queen set her cup down on the silver tray, so hard that its fragile handle cracked in two.

"I will not drink this . . . this vile *poison*," she snapped at the Beauty Consultant.

The Beauty Consultant looked up from his work. He was weaving dried flowers and herbs into a braid, along with strands of eel skin.

"It is one of my finest potions, Your Majesty," the Beauty Consultant replied. Beneath the hooded lids, his eyes flashed yellow.

"I don't care if it is the Elixir of Immortality. I will not drink it. It tastes like sewage," the queen told him.

"Very good, Your Majesty."

"Please make me something else."

"Of course, Your Majesty."

"Something sweet."

"Yes, Your Majesty."

At least he was not lecturing her. The queen rubbed her temples and sighed. This evening had been a disaster from the start. She had asked the cook to make her favorite rabbit stew, with leeks and wild mushrooms, but the cook had disobeyed her, saying that there had not been enough plump rabbits, and made some odious fowl dish instead.

And later Brun and Balto had failed to perform their usual artistry on her. Allegedly recovering from some illness, they had been weak, uninspired, useless. It occurred to her that she should have sent them away for their underperformance and ordered new ones. Perhaps she would do that tomorrow.

And finally . . . she had been expecting Lacan for the last hour. Where was he, anyway? He was never late.

There was a soft knock on the door. *Ah, at last.* Thinking quickly, she took a large red apple from the silver tray and bit into it, to dispel the wretched taste of the tea. Then she stood up and studied herself in the mirror. She smiled, pleased. She looked particularly stunning tonight, in her red silk gown and gold jewelry.

"Come in!" she called out.

The door opened. The queen's smile faded.

It was not Lacan.

"What are *you* doing here?" she demanded.

Andreas entered the chambers and bowed deeply, his head nearly touching the floor. "I beg your pardon, Your Majesty. But it was most urgent that I speak to you as soon as possible."

"It is almost midnight!"

"I apologize, Your Majesty. I have been riding since sundown."

The queen glanced at the Beauty Consultant. He nodded.

"Fine, sit down," the queen ordered Andreas. "But please be brief. I have other business to attend to."

"I understand, Your Majesty." Andreas shrugged off his black wool cloak and sank into a chair. He looked pale, exhausted. "I need to speak to you about your daughter."

"Ana? What has she done now?"

"It is Beauty. She refuses to take it," Andreas explained.

The queen stared at Andreas. "She has not taken it?"

Andreas shook his head. "All the other girls have taken it. And it has worked exactly as you predicted. But your daughter—she has refused most adamantly."

"The little witch," the queen muttered under her breath.

"That is not all. Since arriving at the Academy, Ana has become . . . well, she has taken great interest in her appearance. She has become quite attractive, in fact. And she continues to grow more so every day."

Andreas's words were like a knife piercing her heart. "What?" she cried out. "Are you saying that my daughter is no longer ugly?"

Andreas nodded. "Exactly, Your Majesty. That's why I had to come to you immediately. For further instructions."

The queen began pacing around the room, hugging her chest. The pain in her heart was almost more than she could bear. It was the same pain she had felt years ago, when she had found out about Galen and the girl. It was the same pain she had felt on the occasion of Ana's twelfth birthday, when Ambassador Bertl had seen Ana in her red velvet party dress and remarked, "Your daughter, your little Tatiana, is going to be the greatest beauty in Ran someday. Take my word for it."

Ana was smart—brilliant, even. She had figured out what being beautiful would cost her, as far as the queen was concerned. And she had behaved, for the last four years.

But *something* at the Academy had made Ana

change her mind. Now it was all unraveling.

"What about her friend, Pell?" the queen asked Andreas suddenly.

"She has taken Beauty, Your Majesty. And it has been successful," Andreas replied.

"Has Ana expressed concern about her?"

"Yes, Your Majesty. I fabricated a story that you had dispatched your personal doctor to take care of Pell and the others. I'm not sure Ana was satisfied with that."

"This cannot be happening," the queen said, her voice cracking with fury. "You have failed to do your job, Andreas! And for the extraordinary amount of gold I have paid you—"

Andreas stood up quickly and bowed his head. "Your Majesty! I understand that things may not have gone exactly according to your wishes. I had not anticipated Ana to be so independent-minded. That is why I have come to you. I wish to execute your elegant plan to its conclusion. But I must impose on your great wisdom in order to do so."

The queen narrowed her eyes at him. "And you will do whatever it takes?"

"Yes, Your Majesty. Whatever it takes."

The queen walked over to her dressing table. She opened the top drawer and pulled out a red velvet bag with a gold tassel.

She handed the bag to Andreas. "I believe your instructions will be clear. Do not fail me again."

Andreas took the bag from her and bowed. "You can count on me, Your Majesty."

"Return to me as soon as you have news."

"Of course, Your Majesty."

"Now go. If you start now, you will reach the school by sunrise. Just be careful of the wild boars."

"Yes, Your Majesty."

Andreas picked up his cloak, bowed again, and left.

Queen Veda returned to her chair, ate the rest of the apple, and did not look up to meet the Beauty Consultant's eyes.

25

❦

"I DON'T WANT IT," PELL MUMBLED.

Ana lay down in bed next to Pell and wiped her forehead with a cool, scented cloth. Pell groaned and turned away.

"Pella Bella," Ana whispered. "Are you okay? Are you having a nightmare?"

Pell groaned again. "Momi, make them go away."

"Pella, it's me. Tati."

"No, don't!" Pell cried out.

Ana sat up slightly and took a deep breath. She couldn't rouse Pell from her bad dream. Outside, night birds and insects whirred and chirped. A branch scraped against the windowpane. Somewhere down the hall, a girl began sobbing. Then the sobs subsided.

Ana wished she understood the power Beauty

seemed to have over the girls. She had heard of beauty potions that had terrible side effects. She had read about some of them in her herbology book: a substance called belladonna, which women applied to their eyes to beautify the pupils and which could lead to blindness, and another one called arsenic, which women swallowed in order to improve their skin and which was fatal in large enough doses.

She knew too about more recent beauty potions, such as the ones the Beauty Consultant made for her mother. She had often seen him in the conservatory, harvesting herbs, plucking bugs and worms off of trees, throwing everything into his pockets. She had also seen him leafing through his book, the one with the strange, spidery hieroglyphics and the illustrations of flora and fauna, and muttering happily to himself.

And then there were the distant villages where criminals sold dangerous drugs to commoners, hoping to pass them off as tranquilizers, pleasure-enhancers, beauty tonics. Ana had heard Melk and the other servants at the castle talking about them. Perhaps Andreas had obtained Beauty that way. Perhaps Andreas had intended to help the girls at the Academy become more beautiful, to elevate his popularity even further, and had unknowingly purchased something toxic instead.

Or perhaps not.

The flame of the candle flickered and went out. In the darkness of the room, with only the faint silvery glow of the moon shining through the window, Pell looked eerily gray and still, like a statue.

Ana dipped the cloth in a small pan full of cold water, lavender, and mint. Then she squeezed it out and ran it across Pell's forehead.

This time Pell didn't move or say a word. She had fallen into a deeper layer of sleep, beyond waking, beyond dreams. Beyond Ana.

"It's okay, Pella Bella," Ana whispered. "Tomorrow I am going to ride to the palace and get Momi. She will rid this place of Andreas and his horrible drug. And then everything will be back to normal. I promise you."

She was walking through a cave made of ice and diamonds. Her father was at her side, dressed in bearskin. She was dressed in a long, hooded coat made of white fur. Three white rabbits ran alongside them.

A strange wind blew through the cave, whistling through her hair, chilling her even through her heavy clothing. Icicles tingled like chimes. Diamonds sparkled and shimmered in the lamplight.

She tried to speak. But her father silenced her. "This is a holy place," he whispered. "You must not say or do anything until we reach the end."

The end of what? she wanted to ask him. *What is this cave? And why is it holy?*

Just then the three white rabbits came to a halt and began screaming. It was a terrible sound—the sound of dying.

"Popi!" she cried out. "What's wrong with the rabbits?"

"Stay here," her father ordered her.

Then he was gone—vanished. She was alone with the screaming rabbits.

"Popi, what do I do?" she shouted.

The rabbits continued screaming.

She reached down and scooped the rabbits up in her arms. She knew that they did not like being held, that their spines were fragile, and that they could die if they thrashed and kicked hard enough. Still, she grasped them firmly and rubbed their ears with her chin and whispered soothing words to them: "It's okay. It's all right. I'm going to get you out of here."

The rabbits grew rigid with fear. She could feel them trembling in her arms. "I'm not like her. I won't hurt you," she promised them.

The trembling subsided slightly. She held on to the rabbits tightly and began stumbling through the cave.

The cave was total blackness; she had left her lamp somewhere. As she ran she could feel her bare feet—

where had her boots gone?—scraping against slivers of diamonds and shards of ice. The resulting cuts were excruciating; she could smell her own blood, the scent rising like steam in the frozen air.

But she couldn't stop now. She kept running, running, wondering when the blackness and pain would end.

And then she saw him standing there, at the opening.

"I knew you would find it," he said, smiling.

Ana stopped in front of him, breathless, weeping from the pain. "But why did you tell me to stay?"

"I wanted to see if you would disobey me," he replied.

"What?" Ana said, confused.

The rabbits jumped out of her arms and scattered away, into the sunlight.

"Disobedience is the first sign of a true ruler," her father said.

There was a soft knock on the door. Ana sat up with a gasp and blinked into the pale gray morning light.

Her father was gone. So were the rabbits.

She was in her room. She had been asleep, dreaming.

Ana glanced around and realized that Pell was curled up next to her, her eyes shut tight, her lips moving. Ana reached over and touched her forehead. *Good.* It was cooler than it had been the night before.

There was another knock, louder this time.

"One minute!" Ana called out. Who could it be, at this early hour? It was probably Calla or Nyla or one of the other girls, wandering the halls in their sleep. It was good that she was getting up, anyhow. She had to sneak out to the stables and procure one of the horses for her long journey home.

Being careful not to disturb Pell, Ana rose out of bed and walked over to the mirror. She ran a hand across her dress—the same one from the day before—to smooth the creases. She combed her hair quickly and rubbed the sleep from her eyes.

Finally she opened the door.

It was Andreas.

Ana froze where she stood. What was he doing here? He looked awful, disheveled. His clothes were soaking wet and covered with mud.

Ana did not want to reveal to Andreas that she knew about his getting the other girls addicted to Beauty. It could prove dangerous or otherwise disadvantageous to her.

So she had to improvise. "If you've come to seek an apology for my behavior yesterday in the garden, I don't have one to give," she said in a crisp voice. "In any case, it's too early to be having this conversation."

Andreas shook his head. "It is *I* who wish to apologize.

I made a terrible mistake." His voice was hoarse, ragged.

"*You* wish to apologize?"

"Yes! But first I must speak to you about another, more urgent matter. You see, I have been to see your mother."

Ana gasped. "You have? When?"

"I rode there and back during the night. That is why I—" Andreas waved at his dirty clothes. "In any case, she has a message she wished me to deliver to you."

"What is her message?"

"Come. We must speak in private. She is in trouble."

Ana felt the blood drain out of her face. "Momi is . . . in trouble? What's wrong with her? Please, please, you must tell me!"

"Come with me. In private."

Ana glanced over her shoulder at Pell. She was still asleep.

"Fine, just let me get my shawl," she told Andreas.

"Quickly!"

Ana grabbed her shawl, closed the door softly, and followed Andreas down the hall. He seemed very agitated about something. Ana's heart was pounding in her chest. Was her mother ill? Had she been injured? Was the palace under attack? Now it was more urgent than ever that she get home.

"Outside," Andreas said. He took her arm and

steered her toward the front door. "We must get as far from the building as possible. We cannot risk being overheard by anyone."

"Why not?"

"You'll know soon enough."

Outside, the garden was damp with dew. Birds pecked hungrily at the ground. The sun cast a faint, yellow-gray light across the landscape, making everything look somehow unreal.

Now Andreas was half-walking, half-running, past the irises, past the stone bridge, past the cherry trees. His grip on her arm almost hurt. Ana was beginning to feel even more frightened. She feared the worst. She feared that her mother was in danger, that some terrible political treachery was afoot.

Andreas led her past the maze and into the forest. It was dark and cool and quiet there. Hundreds of tall, ancient trees—older than the Academy, older than Ran itself—formed a thick canopy high over their heads. Ana could not even make out a sliver of sky.

Andreas reached a clearing and turned to Ana. The moss was soft under their feet. Out of the corner of her eye, Ana saw a small brown deer pivot and flee through the trees.

Ana glanced up at Andreas. "Please, won't you tell me now?" she implored him. "There is no one here but us. What is wrong with my mother? What message has she sent to me?"

Andreas stared at her for a long moment. "Forgive me," he said, finally.

"What?"

Andreas reached into the pocket of his cloak. He pulled out a small red velvet bag with a gold tassel.

Ana started. She recognized the bag. She had seen her mother take it out of her dressing table once.

Andreas opened the bag—and pulled out a silver dagger.

Ana's blood froze. "Wh-what are you doing with that?" she stammered.

"Forgive me," Andreas repeated with a sad smile. "But you have become too beautiful for your own good."

Ana screamed. A flock of birds burst out of the trees and scattered into the air.

Before Ana could react, Andreas moved toward her and thrust the silver dagger at her heart. Ana screamed again and grabbed his wrist just before the sharp point of the blade touched her skin.

They struggled. Ana was shocked at her own strength, her will to survive. She kicked Andreas in the shin. He tried to twist her arm behind her.

Then she reached down and bit his hand, hard.

Andreas cried out—and dropped the knife. It landed

in a bed of soft green moss. Ana picked it up quickly.

The knife felt strangely warm in her hand. The handle was heavy and smooth, with the letter *V* carved on it, in old Innish script, for "Veda."

Her mother—her *mother*—had ordered this. The realization pounded through Ana's veins like blood. Her mother was so desperate to be the most beautiful woman in Ran that she would do anything to stay that way. Even if it meant killing her own daughter.

Perhaps it would be better to die, knowing this.

On the other hand, she had to stay on this earth. She had to fight—for Pell, for the others, and most of all, for herself.

"Give me the knife, Ana," Andreas ordered her. "Give it to me now." He lunged toward her.

Ana knew that she was no match for him physically. Thinking quickly she lifted her mother's knife to her face and cut a long slash down her right cheek. She bit down on her lip to keep from crying out. She could taste her blood on her lips, mingling with her tears.

"There," Ana spat out at Andreas as he stared at her in horror. "You can tell my mother that I'm ugly again. She has nothing to worry about. She can let me live."

26

ANA RAN, RAN THROUGH THE WOODS, NOT STOPPING EVEN to see if Andreas was following her. She had no idea if she was going in the right direction; she could barely make out the sun through the treetops. Everything hurt: all the muscles in her body, the hideous cut on her face. But she was beyond pain, beyond crying. She had only one goal in mind.

It all made sense to her now, although "sense" implied rationality, and there was no rationality here. *War is what human beings do to each other when there is no morality left.* Her mother was at war with beautiful young girls. Not just Ana, but all the beautiful young girls in Ran.

Ana realized that the Academy had been a fabrication from the start. Her mother had obviously created it in order to sequester beautiful young girls there, far away from the supervision and vigilance of their families.

Once there, Andreas, under the queen's orders, had encouraged the girls to become even more beautiful by taking Beauty. But Beauty had done the opposite. Ana still had no idea what Beauty was, exactly, except that it had made all the girls sick, weak, and desperately unhappy. It had taken their true beauty away from them.

Her mother—and Andreas—were murderers, or as bad as murderers. And what was Andreas planning to do next? Ana imagined Pell lying in her bed, asleep, unsuspecting, vulnerable. What if Andreas came to her and forced her to take more Beauty?

Ana swiped at her face with the back of her sleeve and hurried her steps. She glanced over her shoulder; Andreas was not following her. *Good.* She had to get to the nearest village and find a horse. It was the only way she could make it to the palace in time.

Queen Veda stared at herself in the mirror. It was fascinating, really, what the Beauty Consultant's newest potions had done for her. Her black hair shone like onyx. Her skin was pearly, almost translucent. And the thin, spidery lines that used to fan out from the corners of her eyes were gone. She looked almost like the young girl she had been when she had first met Galen.

"I must say, your work has been particularly fine lately," she called out to the Beauty Consultant cheerfully. She picked up a jeweled brush and began brushing her hair.

The Beauty Consultant was sitting on his favorite stool. He was plucking the petals of a peculiar-looking green flower and humming to himself. He didn't respond.

"Are you listening to me? I am giving you a compliment," the queen said, more loudly.

He still didn't respond. She turned to frown at him. Beneath their hooded eyelids, his eyes glowed yellow.

"What *is* it?" the queen demanded. "Why have you been acting like this all day? Did Andreas's visit last night trouble you? He is irrelevant."

"He may be irrelevant, Your Majesty. But what you ordered him to do is not," the Beauty Consultant stated simply.

The queen sighed. Why did he insist on being so annoying? "You have no right to be sanctimonious with me. You are the one who has been telling me all along that she is my biggest threat."

"That is true, Your Majesty. However, I never said anything about—"

The queen threw her hairbrush at him. It missed him and hit the wall behind him. It broke, sending shards flying through the air.

"*Stop* it! Just stop it. Be silent, I order you!" she shouted.

The Beauty Consultant's eyes turned from yellow to black. "As you wish, Your Majesty."

"And bring me another hairbrush!"

"As you wish, Your Majesty."

Just then the door burst open. The queen glanced up, startled that anyone would dare to enter her chambers without knocking.

A girl was standing there.

No, not a girl. *Ana.*

The queen felt as though she would faint, so violent was the shock that shook her body. How—*how*—could Ana be alive? Why had Andreas not followed her orders?

"Hello, Momi," Ana said. She was not smiling.

Andreas had been right. Ana looked like her old self, before everything, before the time after her twelfth birthday. Gone were the greasy, ragged hair, the mottled skin, the dirty clothes.

There was, however, a long, bloody gash down her face.

Ana walked up to her and stood over her where she sat. The Beauty Consultant dropped his green flower and stared at Ana.

The queen finally managed to find her voice. "What are you doing here? You are supposed to be . . . you are supposed to be at school!"

"I know what you have been doing, Momi."

"Answer me! Why are you here?" the queen demanded.

"I know why you started the Academy, and why you sent all those girls there. I know what Andreas has been doing, with those pink pills. You can't keep any secrets from me anymore."

"You are speaking nonsense," the queen said, laughing shrilly. "Where are your manners, Ana? You are being foolish and disrespectful. I am going to send for the guards and have you taken back to the Academy immediately."

Ana moved closer to her mother. "You're going back to the Academy with me, Momi," she said in a steely voice. "You're going to stop what's happening there. You're going to get those girls out of there and have them taken to the hospital. Some of them are very sick. Including Pell. It's the least you can do, considering that you tried to have me killed."

The queen stared at Ana in bewilderment. When had her pathetic, helpless, needy little daughter become such an upstart, a troublemaker?

But it didn't matter. Ana was not going to stop her now.

"I am not here to listen to your orders, much less follow them," she snapped. "You are a stupid, ugly little fool. Despite all your play-acting, despite all your window-dressing, *I* am the queen. *I* am the most beautiful woman in Ran."

She smiled at the Beauty Consultant, waiting for his confirmation. He stood up and regarded her. His hooded eyes were black.

"Well?" the queen said impatiently.

Then the Beauty Consultant turned to Ana. His eyes began to glow blue, then green, then a deep, fiery red.

"It is as I predicted," he whispered, so softly that the queen could barely hear him. "She has surpassed you."

"*What?* You idiot, what are you talking about?"

"She is now the fairest woman in the kingdom," the Beauty Consultant pronounced.

The queen leaped across the room and lunged at the Beauty Consultant. He stood there, not moving, not resisting. She wrapped her hands around his tiny, wrinkly neck and began squeezing, squeezing, as hard as she could.

"You are *lying*! You are a *liar*!" she screamed.

She felt Ana grab her from behind. "Momi, stop it!" she shouted. "Stop it, you're killing him!"

In response, the queen squeezed the Beauty Consultant's neck even harder. Her knuckles turned white; her fingers were bleeding. Her efforts seemed to have no effect on him, though. He merely stood there and stared at her with his cold, black, inscrutable eyes.

"You are a *liar*!" the queen screamed at him. "You are a *liar*, and a *traitor*, and you must *die*!"

"Momi!"

The Beauty Consultant continued to stare at her. "I'm sorry, Your Majesty. But your reign is over," he whispered. Then his lips curled up in a hint of a smile.

It was too much for her to bear. The pain in her heart—the pain that she had been carrying for so very long—exploded and spread through her body in hot waves. She touched her chest—she couldn't breathe, she couldn't breathe. What was happening to her? Why did she hurt so much?

And then she saw Galen standing over her. "I did love you, once," he murmured. "It's such a shame."

"What are you doing here? You're supposed to be dead! I killed you myself!" she yelled at him.

"You cannot kill me," he replied. But it was the Beauty Consultant who had spoken.

And then Ana's face swam into her field of vision: Ana's lovely, beautiful face with its long red battle scar. "Dearest Momi, rest in peace," she said, tears streaming down her cheeks.

"No!" the queen shouted.

But she was already dead.

27

❧

THE MORNING WAS GRAY AND COOL, WITH THE PROMISE OF rain. Doves fluttered around the gravesite, pecking at the ground, cooing softly.

"May peace be with you as you join your family— your beloved husband and your mother and your father—in their eternal rest," said the royal priest. He made the sign of the heavens with his hand, and murmured a silent prayer.

Ana stood very still and watched as the thirteen young soldiers lowered her mother into the freshly dug earth. Stefan was among them. So was Lacan.

There was no visible sign of emotion on Lacan's face. He did, however, turn to acknowledge her with a bow of his head. He had been one of the soldiers she had led to the Academy after her mother's death, to arrest

Andreas and free the remaining girls. Including Pell.

Pell leaned over and touched Ana's arm. "Are you okay, Tati?" she whispered.

"I'm fine," Ana whispered back. "Thank you for being here."

"Tati! There was no way I wasn't going to be here!"

Ana squeezed Pell's hand gratefully. Pell was still thin and pale, but getting better every day. The week's stay at the hospital had helped to undo the effects of Beauty and restore much of her former health. Most of the other girls had been released as well. Only a few of them, including Lilika, who had taken the pills for the longest, were being kept for several more days.

Ana glanced over her shoulder. Just behind them were Omi and all the other palace staff members—and behind them, hundreds of dignitaries and heads of territories who had come to pay their respects to the dead queen. Omi frowned sternly at Ana. Ana knew that look. She should have worn a warm shawl over her pink lace dress—or better yet, worn proper funeral attire.

The Beauty Consultant was nowhere to be seen. He was probably in the conservatory hunting for medicinal insects, Ana thought. Which was just as well. Since the day of her mother's death, she had not been able to face him. Part of her blamed him for what had happened. Of course, part of her blamed herself.

Perhaps the queen would be alive today if she, Ana, had continued eating cloudberry pastries and wearing the servants' clothes.

Although, there was another part of her—a small, dark, shadow part—that was glad that the queen was dead. How could such evil, such hatred, have been allowed to live?

Instinctively Ana reached up and touched her scar. It would be with her forever, a symbol of what she had done to survive for so many years.

"Your Majesty."

Ana started. The priest was talking. To her.

"Yes, Father Nuri?"

The priest bowed deeply. "Your Majesty, if you would initiate the final part of the ceremony."

"Of course, Father."

He handed her a silver bowl full of red and white rose petals. She took it from him and walked to the edge of her mother's open grave.

Below, Queen Veda looked so still and peaceful. She wore a long black velvet gown with a light brown collar and buttons made of onyx and velvet. Around her neck was a diamond necklace that her mother, the Lady Despina, had passed on to her when she died. The Beauty Consultant had performed his final duty to her by dressing the queen for the occasion. He had also painted her face in a ceremonial death mask. He had made her look . . . beautiful.

The priest murmured another prayer. Ana took a deep breath and scattered the rose petals across her mother's body.

"May the pink angels visit your dreams," Ana whispered.

Then she stepped aside to let the soldiers with the shovels finish their work.

EPILOGUE

And so began the long and happy rule of Queen Tatiana Anatolia, the third ruler of the royal kingdom of Ran. With her friend Pell Fortunas at her side as the head of the royal guards, she would be forever known as the queen who liberated the young women of the Academy and restored order to the land.